1⁵⁰

Lost and Found

....
Judy Baer

Cedar River Daydreams

1 • New Girl in Town
2 • Trouble with a Capital "T"
3 • Jennifer's Secret
4 • Journey to Nowhere
5 • Broken Promises
6 • The Intruder
7 • Silent Tears No More
8 • Fill My Empty Heart
9 • Yesterday's Dream
10 • Tomorrow's Promise
11 • Something Old, Something New
12 • Vanishing Star
13 • No Turning Back
14 • Second Chance
15 • Lost and Found
16 • Unheard Voices

Other Books by Judy Baer

• Paige
• Adrienne

Lost and Found

Judy Baer

BETHANY HOUSE PUBLISHERS
MINNEAPOLIS, MINNESOTA 55438

Lost and Found
Judy Baer

Library of Congress Catalog Card Number 91–77737

ISBN 1–55661–243–5

Published by Bethany House Publishers
A Ministry of Bethany Fellowship, Inc.
6820 Auto Club Road, Minneapolis, Minnesota 55438

Printed in the United States of America

For Amy M.,
my "almost" niece

JUDY BAER received a B.A. in English and Education from Concordia College in Moorhead, Minnesota. She has had over nineteen novels published and is a member of the National Romance Writers of America, the Society of Children's Book Writers and the National Federation of Press Women.

Two of her novels, *Adrienne* and *Paige*, have been prizewinning bestsellers in the Bethany House SPRINGFLOWER SERIES (for girls 12–15). Both books have been awarded first place for juvenile fiction in the National Federation of Press Women's communications contest.

In all these things

we are more than conquerors

through him who loved us.

ROMANS 8:37

Chapter One

Though Egg and Binky McNaughton, Jennifer Golden, and Peggy Madison had come to Lexi Leighton's house to study, not much homework was getting done. Todd Winston's presence was to blame.

It was Todd's second outing from the hospital since the night of the football accident that had so gravely injured him. He had been released for an evening once before in order to talk to the church youth group about the struggles he'd gone through after his injury. Today, though, Todd was at Lexi's house—just like old times! No doubt about it, a celebration was in order.

Egg glanced at his "cartoon character" watch. "What time did you say you had to go back to the hospital?"

"My parents will pick me up in an hour." Todd smiled at the familiar, concerned faces of his friends. "When the physical therapist suggested that my parents take me home for the afternoon, I wasn't sure it would be a good idea. Now I realize this is the best medicine."

"I wish you didn't have to go back," Binky complained. "It's so great to have you with us. We've missed you."

"And I've missed being here. It won't be long now, though, before I'll be released for good. Actually, I think my mom is relieved that I'm still in the hospital." He glanced ruefully at the shiny aluminum walker parked near his chair. "Every time I take off in that thing or on my crutches, Mom acts like she's going to have a heart attack. She's afraid I'll fall and end up where I started."

"But that couldn't happen, could it?" Binky asked. She and the others had been at the hospital the night they'd learned Todd might be permanently paralyzed. They were all thrilled to know his injuries were not as serious as they first appeared.

"You know how mothers are." Todd looked at the cluster of girls and the comical, concerned expression of his best friend, Egg. "Sometimes I feel like there are a half-dozen of them around me."

The girls ignored the comment.

"I didn't know you were using crutches," Jennifer piped. "That's progress, isn't it?"

"It sure is. I'll be able to maneuver around the school more easily than I'd expected." He grimaced. "Still, I'd rather be moving around on my own strength."

"Is that possible?" Peggy ventured.

"Anything's possible!" Lexi said with an enthusiastic grin. "Look how fast Todd's improved so far. He's amazed the doctors."

Todd flexed the muscles in his arms, showing well-developed biceps. "I exercise more hours a day in the hospital than I ever did when I was quarterback." His grin wavered slightly. "And if I have anything to say about it, I'll be quarterback again."

The group was silent. That was a big dream considering the injuries Todd had sustained.

"I can't imagine wanting to be quarterback again if I'd nearly broken my neck in a football accident," Jennifer said bluntly, tossing her blond hair away from her eyes and cracking her gum loudly.

"I agree," Peggy said. "Why would you want to go back for more?" The vivid image of Todd's broken body sprawled on the football field was still clear in her mind.

"I don't know. Maybe it's like they say: 'When the horse bucks you off, the first thing to do is get back on and ride again.' I need to conquer my fears. It would be easy to baby myself and never take part in sports or physical activities again. That's my fear talking. Common sense tells me it's good for me to exercise and move my body."

"But as *quarterback?*" Binky interjected doubtfully.

Lexi had been silent for a while. Todd caught her gaze with his own as he spoke. "I know. I know. It sounds crazy. I've had nightmares about the accident. I still have them occasionally when things haven't been going well with my physical therapy or when I get overtired. But we all have to set goals and attempt to achieve them. Maybe I won't ever be quarterback again. Maybe the most I'll ever be is Egg's co-manager for the football team. But that's great, because the job is important and takes plenty of hard work. I would still feel as though I were accomplishing something."

Todd's brilliant smile lit the room. "I'm thankful to God for being here; for being alive and able to feel and move my hands and feet. Sometimes when I'm alone in the hospital, I just lie there and wiggle my toes and grin."

Binky giggled. Her face flushed pink. Soon she was clutching her sides and laughing hysterically.

"What did I say that was so funny?" Todd wondered aloud.

Binky wiped the tears from her eyes. "It just occurred to me that sometimes my brother Egg likes to lie in bed and wiggle his toes and grin, too. But with Egg it's some sort of *mental* exercise. I guess he's checking to make sure his feet and brain are still connected."

Egg froze, his hand poised over the bowl of tortilla chips. "Very funny, Binky. Hilarious. Uproarious. Hysterical."

Binky grinned smugly. "I thought so."

Egg scowled at his sister and stuffed a tortilla chip in his mouth. Then he bit the corner off another and started to dip it into the salsa.

"Egg, don't do that!" Binky barked.

"What? What'd I do now?" Egg demanded.

"You took a *bite* of that chip and were just about to dip it in the salsa. It's disgusting."

"Oh." Egg looked blank. "I didn't realize I'd done that. You're being weird again, Binky," he added indignantly. "We're with friends, after all." He looked at Lexi, Todd, Jennifer, and Peggy. "Let's take a poll. How many of you think it's gross to dip a tortilla chip in salsa twice?" No one said a word, and Egg suddenly blushed to the roots of his hair. "Oh, never mind. It was a stupid question. Sorry, Binky. I'll never do that again."

Egg's retreat was amazing, certainly unexpected. Todd looked at him and then at Binky, at Lexi, and back again. "What's going on here?" he quizzed. "I don't think I've ever heard you apologize to your sister, Egg."

"Did Pastor Lake have something to do with it?" Lexi asked, grinning slyly.

Everyone in the room understood. Pastor Lake was the new youth pastor at Lexi's church. Since he'd come to town, Egg and Binky had become Christians and joined the church.

"We think it would be a good idea if we didn't fight quite so much," Egg admitted.

Binky nodded in agreement.

"The trouble is, we've discovered that what Binky and I really like to do is argue . . ."

" . . . with each other!" Binky added.

"We think it's fun." Egg smiled. "Do you think we're crazy?"

Lexi, Todd, Jennifer, and Peggy all burst into laughter.

"I don't think the kind of fighting you and Binky do is harmful," Todd decided.

"I agree," Peggy added. "It's more like your way of . . ."

" . . . communicating," Todd finished the sentence for her.

"Exactly. Other people talk; you argue."

"Well, I'm glad to hear you see it that way," Binky admitted. "I've been trying to be patient, but sometimes I feel like exploding when Egg says or does something ridiculous. I have to learn to keep my mouth shut sometimes."

"I think you should be congratulated for trying," Lexi said, smiling at both her friends. "I'm impressed."

"I am too," Jennifer agreed. "Although, I must admit it doesn't really seem normal not to have you bickering all the time."

"A for effort!" Todd declared.

They all knew Egg and Binky loved each other very much, whether they were fighting or not. Lexi had a hunch this phase would pass. Soon Egg and Binky would fall back into their familiar pattern of affectionate bickering. It was the way they related best, even though each would "walk through fire" for the other.

"You know what?" Jennifer said. "I'm really impressed with what Pastor Lake's done for the youth group. It's not just Egg's and Binky's lives he's touched."

"That's for sure. The group is really booming. Everyone loved the scavenger hunt and the 'Search for Christians' party. You'll enjoy youth group, Todd," Egg assured his friend, "more than ever."

Todd turned to Jennifer, who sat in the recliner across from him. "Has Matt Windsor been coming to the group?"

Jennifer snorted and Binky giggled. "Matt who?" she asked, feigning ignorance.

"Sorry I asked," Todd said, unsuccessfully repressing a smile.

Matt and Jennifer were obviously "off" in their "on again/off again" relationship.

"Men," Jennifer muttered. She lifted her pert nose disdainfully. "Excuse me," she corrected, "I mean *boys*. They're hardly worth the trouble they cause."

"I'd certainly agree with that." Binky glared at Egg as he continued to munch on the tortilla chips, dipping an occasional one more than once into the salsa. "For one thing, they aren't very bright. They *never* seem to learn."

Egg smiled benignly at his sister and chewed away nonchalantly.

"Sometimes I think the world would have been a better place if men hadn't been put on the planet." The playful tone of the others was not reflected in Peggy's voice. It had a sharp, bitter edge. Her eyes clouded over, glittering with unshed tears.

Egg wiped his hands on his jeans. "You can't mean that, Peggy," he protested. "Just because Jennifer is mad at Matt, and Binky doesn't like the way I eat tortilla chips . . ." He stopped short, unable to finish the sentence.

"You can't count on men for anything," Peggy continued, lost in her own thoughts. "Give them a chance and they'll disappoint you." Peggy was especially vulnerable since the suicide death of her boyfriend, Chad Allen. She was usually a bundle of nerves, easily upset by the simplest, innocent conversation.

Lexi got up to switch tapes in the cassette player. She stared sadly at her friend. Since she'd first met her, Peggy had changed in many ways. Before Chad's death, she'd been pregnant with his child and given the baby up for adoption. Then, because Peggy had broken off their relationship, she felt Chad's suicide was her fault.

Now Peggy's life seemed to be in new turmoil. She'd become very argumentative. Rather than let innocent comments pass in conversation, she often took issue with them.

"Men think they're so smart," she blurted, "yet they're the cause of all the trouble—family problems, the economy, war. The world's a mess."

"I don't want to take the blame for all that," Egg protested mildly, trying to pacify Peggy.

She would not be deterred. "Men don't think before they act. They're impulsive and irresponsible."

As the spirited, one-sided conversation continued, Lexi recalled the times she'd overheard Peggy arguing with her parents, with teachers at school, and with her friends.

"Relax, Peggy," Todd soothed. "Men aren't so bad. Take your dad, for example. He's a great guy."

"Not all men are careless with money, war hungry, or responsible for family break-ups," added Egg.

A weary expression crossed Peggy's features. She flopped backward against her chair. With a dismissing wave of her hand, she said, "Forget it. Just forget it. I'm too tired to argue about it."

Everyone was surprised to see Peggy give in so easily. Lately, her argumentive moods lasted longer. Then as quickly as they began, she'd move from mad to happy; from melancholy to oddly animated.

Something was wrong with Peggy—the mood swings, the arguments, the blurry-eyed unfocused lack of concentration she sometimes displayed. Her short attention span irritated her friends, as did her often impulsive, thoughtless behavior.

Peggy Madison was a tall, strong, athletic girl.

Lately, however, Lexi had noticed an unusual clumsiness about her. It was as though something in Peggy gave way when Chad died. Lexi longed for a way to mend the damage.

Lexi's thoughts skittered to a conversation she'd had with Peggy's mother.

"She's a different girl. She's secretive and irritable," Mrs. Madison had said. *"Sometimes I don't feel I know her anymore. She spends so much time in her room. Do you think as her friend you could do something to draw her out?"*

Lexi had promised to try, but in spite of her efforts she felt that Peggy was drifting away. Once they had been very close. They'd cried, prayed, and laughed together. No more. Hard as it was to admit, Lexi felt like a stranger around her friend.

"I've brought treats!" a cheerful voice interrupted Lexi's thoughts. Her little brother Benjamin stood in the doorway, cradling a huge bowl in his arms. "Benjamin and Mom made caramel corn. Want some?"

Lexi heard the relieved sighs of her friends. Ben's entrance had shattered the tension in the room.

"Benjamin," Jennifer said, "you're getting so tall!"

"Ben's growing up," he agreed. "See my pants?" He stuck one leg forward to show the hem of his jeans. It touched the top of his sock.

"Are those your high-water pants?" Lexi teased.

Ben laughed. "My pants shrunk in the flood!

"I'm tall." Ben settled the bowl of popcorn on the table and patted his stomach. "And thin. See?" He turned sideways to display his flat tummy. Though Ben and Lexi's friends probably weren't aware of it,

Lexi knew her mother monitored Benjamin's eating habits closely. Ben was born with Down's syndrome, and had a tendency to gain weight easily. But he was trim and fit, and proud of his physical abilities, taking part in all the athletic events at the Academy for the Handicapped.

"Ben's a big hit with the girls at school," Lexi confided with a smile. "He's awfully handsome, don't you think?"

Benjamin's almond-shaped eyes sparkled with delight, and he ruffled his own silky dark hair in embarrassment. It was impossible to dislike Ben. He radiated charm and personality.

"So, what's going on at the Academy, Ben?" Todd asked. "Have you learned anything new?"

The question invoked a lengthy description of science experiments and art projects in which Ben had been involved.

"Do you have a girlfriend yet?" Egg quipped.

Ben blushed shyly. "I'm too young for girlfriends," he told Egg, wagging his finger in his face.

Egg wagged a finger right back. "That doesn't mean there aren't girls that like you, Ben. I'll bet there are lots of them."

Ben blushed more deeply. "All of them."

Lexi and Todd burst out laughing. "No self-image problems there," Todd muttered.

"How's your rabbit, Benjamin?" Peggy joined the conversation.

"Bunny's fine. Do you want to see him?"

"When I'm ready to go home, you can show me. Is that all right?"

Ben nodded. "Bunny's going to be our school mascot," he said proudly. "We're going to read about *Uncle Wiggly, Alice in Wonderland,* and *Peter Cottontail.*"

"Sounds like a good year to me, Ben," Egg commented.

Suddenly Ben's animated face was serious. No one spoke as he stepped closer to Todd. He stood by the walker and stared at the metal frame. After a long moment, he touched the cool metal with one small finger.

"Will you use this forever, Todd?"

"Not forever, Ben. In physical therapy they're teaching me to use crutches."

"Crunches?" The word was unfamiliar to him. "What are crunches?"

"*Crutches*, Ben. They're sticks with handles on them to help me keep my balance when I walk."

"But when will you walk like you used to walk?"

Everyone was quiet. They'd all wondered the same thing, but didn't dare ask, knowing how much it frustrated Todd that he wasn't already walking on his own.

"Hopefully by the end of this month I'll be using the *crunches* most of the time. That's when the doctor says I'll be able to leave the hospital and go back to school. I don't know when I'll get rid of the crutches, Ben. It might be a long time."

"How long is a long time?" Ben persisted.

"It could be weeks, months . . . maybe years."

"Years?" Binky gasped.

"My legs are still pretty weak. I may end up with a permanent limp." Todd's jaw tightened. "But if there's any way I can improve my chances of walking without crutches by working hard in physical therapy, I'm going to do it."

The doorbell punctuated Todd's determined statement.

Ben raced to the door and pulled it open. Jerry Randall stood in the doorway, a large poster in his hand. He waved it to catch everyone's attention.

"What've you got there?" Egg went to the door to check out the poster.

"Mrs. Waverly stopped by the Hamburger Shack and asked me to put this in the window."

"Oh . . . then why did you bring it here?"

"I thought you all might be interested." Jerry stepped inside. "It's about the school play."

"Really?" Lexi was intrigued.

Binky groaned. "Remember the melodrama that was supposed to be so funny?"

"It *was* funny," Egg retorted.

"But not for the right reasons," Binky added. "Tim Anders got so carried away he fell off the stage and landed in the orchestra pit."

"That wasn't the worst of it," Peggy said. "He broke his arm and his collarbone. He had to walk around school with a huge cast. Remember?"

"I remember." Binky smiled smugly. "He kept running into people. He turned around too fast once and gave Egg a black eye."

"What play did Mrs. Waverly decide on?"

With a jerk of his hand, Jerry let the poster unroll, then held it up for all to see. The title was emblazoned in large script: *Macbeth.*

"Shakespeare!" someone blurted.

Everyone in the room groaned. "Why *Shakespeare?*"

Binky sat on the floor and began to moan. "I can't *read* Shakespeare. I can't *understand* Shakespeare. How could I be in a Shakespearean play?"

"Why couldn't she pick a play with language that we can all understand?" Jennifer looked indignant. "I'm dyslexic. I can't read ordinary words, let alone Shakespeare!"

Todd chuckled. "Maybe that's exactly why she chose it."

"Huh?" All eyes turned to him.

"Listen to yourselves. You were excited about the play until you heard it was Shakespeare. Now you're moaning and groaning like it's the end of the world. Maybe Mrs. Waverly decided the best way to calm our misgivings about Shakespeare was to involve us in one of his plays."

"How can you be sure about that?" Binky demanded.

"My mom loves to read Shakespeare. She attributes it to an English teacher in high school who directed them in a Shakespearean play," Todd explained.

"But Mrs. Waverly teaches music. Why didn't she pick a musical?"

"I don't know. Maybe she struck a deal with the English department." Todd grinned. "I think it's going to be great."

"Is *Macbeth* a comedy?" Egg wondered aloud. "I wouldn't mind doing it if it's funny."

Lexi burst out laughing. "Sorry, Egg. *Macbeth* is anything but a comedy. It's a tragedy set in eleventh-century Scotland. Macbeth was a warrior who wanted to be king."

"Oh, terrific. That sounds like a lot of fun," Egg moaned drearily.

"It's not so bad. There're some witches in the story, and lots of battle scenes."

"Battle scenes?" That piqued Egg's interest.

"When are the tryouts?" Lexi asked Jerry.

"I'm not sure. You and Todd have had parts before, haven't you?"

"Yeah." Todd pointed to his walker. "But I think I'll pass this year. This thing could detract from the scenery."

"Well, the rest of us could give it a try," Lexi said in an effort to sound positive.

"Are there many parts for girls?" Binky asked.

"There's Lady Macbeth," Todd said. "And, of course, the three witches."

"Yuck," Jennifer groaned. "I don't like witches."

"Shakespeare depicts them as symbols of evil," Todd explained.

"M-m-m-m." Binky nodded. "Speaking of evil, do you think the Hi-Fives will try out for parts?"

"I wonder if Mrs. Waverly is directing it alone?" Todd asked, ignoring Binky's comment about the exclusive girl's club.

"Mr. Raddis is her assistant," Jerry confirmed.

"There's always plenty to do with the sets, publicity, and costuming," Peggy commented. "Sometimes we wonder if anything good will come out of the chaos, but on opening night we're always surprised at how great it turns out."

"The students do all the costuming?" Lexi's eyes

brightened as her imagination ran ahead. "The players for *Macbeth* should have great costumes. Military garb for Macbeth himself, a flowing white robe for Lady Macbeth . . . of course, the witches would wear wispy wigs and smoky gray costumes."

"You'd be good on costumes," Egg said with a smile.

Lexi nodded. "I'm wondering if a Shakespearean play could be as fun as a musical?"

"You bet, Lexi," said Todd. "But it will be hard to top the musical we were in together when you first moved to town."

Todd's comment jolted a flood of memories. Lexi and Todd had had the lead parts. Then she thought of Minda Hannaford's attempt to ruin the evening by stealing Lexi's beautiful costume. Somehow it didn't seem as tragic now as it had at the time.

"If this play even comes close to being as fun as that musical was, it'll be great," she concluded.

There was new energy and excitement among them as the gang discussed the upcoming event.

Chapter Two

"What's going on over there?" Jennifer pointed toward the end of the hallway. A large crowd had gathered by the school's main bulletin board.

"I don't know. I just got here," Lexi said. "Let's get our books and find out."

"Whatever it is, it must be big," Jennifer commented as they made their way toward the growing crowd.

"I see Egg and Binky are right in the middle of it. There's Anna Marie, Tim Anders, and Minda, of course," Lexi said.

Everyone was talking animatedly as the two girls approached. A poster identical to the one Jerry had brought to Lexi's last night was tacked to the board. "Everyone's discovered we're going to do *Macbeth*." Lexi and Jennifer squeezed in closer to hear the conversation.

"*Macbeth?* I've never heard of it!"

"I thought we'd do a comedy again."

"Or a musical."

"Shakespeare's boring. Who'll come to see that?"

There was an outbreak of laughter. "Just about everybody."

"Cedar River High School doing *Macbeth*? It'll be a comedy for sure!"

"I think it will be very intellectually stimulating," Tressa Williams announced to the crowd. "It's time we did something with some challenge."

Tressa tended to flaunt the fact that she was unusually bright. As soon as she put her stamp of approval on the play, the other Hi-Fivers agreed.

"It's definitely a good choice."

"Finally, something interesting."

"A worthwhile plot for a change."

There wasn't a lot of space for original thought in the Hi-Five Club. What one person expressed, they all adopted—whether they truly agreed or not.

Minda Hannaford stood at the head of the crowd, studying the poster intently. Then she tossed her hair over her shoulder in a theatrical gesture.

"Well, I know that *I* for one am going to be in this play . . ." She paused for dramatic effect. ". . . and I'm going to get a significant part." Minda threw back her shoulders confidently and raised her pert nose in the air. "I hear there's a Mrs. Macbeth . . . that's who I'll be."

Tim Anders smirked. "It's *Lady* Macbeth, Minda."

"Whatever. The part will be perfect for me. Where do I sign up?"

"Here's the list for tryouts," someone said. "You can be first, Minda."

"Does anyone know the names of any other characters in the play?"

"Macbeth, Lady Macbeth, Banquo, Macduff."

"Did you say Mac*Duck*?"

"No, silly. Mac*duff*."

Several separated themselves from the group to sign their names on the tryout sheet.

"What about you?" Jennifer turned to Lexi. "Are you going to sign up?"

Lexi glanced at the pressing crowd, the bright poster on the wall, and chewed thoughtfully on her lower lip. "I don't know."

"What's wrong?" Jennifer sounded surprised. "You're the first to try out everything."

"Much as I hate to admit it, I'm not sure Shakespeare will be much fun."

Jennifer's eyes narrowed. "Are you *sure* that's the reason?"

Lexi felt a warm blush creep up her neck. "Actually, I'd hoped the next play I was in would be with Todd again. Do you think that's crazy?"

"I'm sure he'd be happy if you signed up, Lexi. There'll always be another time for you to be in a play together," Jennifer encouraged. "Do you think it's possible he'll return to school before the performance?"

"I don't know. But even if he does, what could he do? He's certainly not able to get around very quickly. I'm afraid Todd's only role this year will be as a spectator."

"I still can't believe it." Jennifer shook her head. "There's actually something that you aren't totally enthusiastic about. You surprise me, Lexi."

Lexi surprised herself. Normally she loved to perform. The musical group, the Emerald Tones, was a great experience for her. Now, when she had the opportunity to use her acting abilities, she hung back.

Surely there was something about *Macbeth* that would interest and energize her!

Egg and Binky pushed their way through the crowd to Lexi and Jennifer.

"We signed up! What are you two waiting for? I've never been in a school play before." Binky's eyes glittered with anticipation. "I hope I get to be in this one. I can hardly wait until tryouts."

"Come on, Lexi." Jennifer poked her in the arm. "Let's do it."

"I don't know . . ." Lexi couldn't get excited about it. She could only think of the million ways she could make a fool of herself doing Shakespeare in a high-school production. She glanced around, hoping for a way out of the uncomfortable predicament.

Then Lexi noticed someone standing in the hall looking even less enthusiastic than she felt. Peggy leaned against the lockers, an angry frown marring her pretty features.

"Looks like Peggy doesn't want to be in *Macbeth* either," Lexi told Jennifer.

"She's really been hanging back, hasn't she?"

"I miss the old Peggy," Binky interjected. "When Chad died, it was as if something in Peggy died, too."

Lexi thought Binky couldn't have said it better. Peggy had begun to do the unexpected, and make inappropriate comments. Right now she just looked miserably unhappy, staring at the excited students signing up for tryouts.

Lexi moved through the crowd toward her friend. "Hi, Peggy, what's up?"

Peggy nodded toward the others. "Big excitement, huh?"

"Are you going to try out for the play?"

"I don't know." Peggy's expression was one of disinterest.

"It might be good for you, Peggy. It would certainly take your mind off everything else that's been going on. I can't imagine anything more taxing than trying to memorize Shakespeare." Lexi gave a weak little laugh. "Frankly, it terrifies me."

"You? I can't believe you'd be terrified about anything."

"Believe it," Lexi replied, frowning. "Jennifer wants me to sign up, but I'm just not sure I can do it."

Suddenly an idea occurred to Lexi. "I'd need some moral support to be involved in a play like this. How about it, Peggy? Would you go out for it with me?"

Peggy crossed her arms and looked at Lexi incredulously. "*With* you? That doesn't make sense, Lexi. You're the most confident girl I know."

"Not when it comes to Shakespeare. I know I'll regret it if I don't offer to help with production or something, but it'd be so much easier if you do it, too."

"Me, *your* moral support? That's a switch."

Lexi rested a hand on Peggy's arm. "Come on. Let's sign up. All we have to do is attend tryouts. We can decide later about actually being in the play or production . . . or maybe Mrs. Waverly will decide for us."

There was a time when Peggy would have been the first to sign up. Now, reluctantly, and only because Lexi coaxed her, she said reluctantly. "I suppose I could check it out."

"That's the spirit. We've got nothing to lose, right?"

"I guess not," Peggy said with a pouty look. "I feel like I've lost everything already."

The first bell rang sharply just as they finished signing the tryout sheet. Peggy hurried toward the classroom.

"Did you sign up?" Binky asked, coming up on Lexi's right elbow.

"We both did," Lexi replied, gesturing toward Peggy's back.

"Great! It's going to be a lot of fun. I hope I get a part," Binky chirped. "How come you're so gloomy-looking, Lexi?"

"I'm hoping I didn't make a mistake," Lexi said.

"What do you mean?"

"I talked Peggy into signing up for tryouts. She didn't want to."

"Peggy hasn't *wanted* to do anything for a long time," Binky pointed out. "She's been depressed and withdrawn beyond normal. It's time she came out of her shell. You did the right thing, Lexi."

———

By the time the final bell of the day rang, Binky was bouncing off the walls.

"Settle down, will you, Binky?" her brother commanded. "All day you've been acting like a kid. Try to sit still without squirming."

"Oh, Egg, you're no fun. Can't you *feel* it? Can't you see what an important day this is?"

Lexi and Jennifer exchanged doubtful glances. What had gotten into Binky now?

"The energy!" Binky enthused. "All because of the play! Don't you understand?"

"Frankly, I'd be terrified if I ever began to understand you, Binky," Egg said.

Binky struck a dramatic pose, her history book resting on one hip, an arm extended high in the air. "It's time for tryouts in just half an hour. Look out *Macbeth*, here I come."

"She's positive she's going to be a star," Egg explained to Jennifer and Lexi.

"There's no doubt about it," Binky concurred. "All the really big actors do Shakespeare first. Do you realize what an advantage it'll be that I'll have already done Shakespeare before I'm out of high school?" She dropped her books to the floor and struck another tragi-comic pose with her hands folded serenely over her chest. "Romeo, Romeo, wherefore art thou, Romeo?"

"You'll be a star all right," Egg agreed. "A *fallen* star. There's no guarantee that you'll get a part in this play, Binky. And even if you do, what makes you think you'll be any good? And even if you are, who do you think of any importance is going to be in the audience to discover you?"

Binky turned melancholic. "Oh, the woes of an aspiring actress." She looked at Egg with pity. "We artists must pay our dues. We may go undiscovered for a time."

Egg looked completely baffled. "I can't talk any sense into her. She's absolutely certain she's going to be the star of this production, and that it'll start her on the path to Broadway. Can any of *you* say something to bring her back to reality?"

"Who knows, Egg? Maybe she's right," Jennifer said with an impish grin.

"Don't encourage her," Egg pleaded. "I've been trying to convince her that she'd be better off working on costumes or makeup. That's where it's at in the industry. There are only a few stars, but every play or movie needs a good production crew. I think it'd be great to be in charge of props or lighting. Especially for a play like *Macbeth*. I hear it has lots of thunderstorms and dark, dreary scenes. Now *there's* an important job. It takes some creativity."

"Bor-rr-ring!" Binky interjected. "Very, very boring."

"It is not." Egg's face flushed pink. "Just because production doesn't get all the credit the actors do, doesn't mean it's not important. I think the production people should come out and take a bow at the end of the play."

Binky shook her head. "But they don't. They just thank all those who 'did so much work to make the production possible.' Then the stars take another bow. I want to be one of the actresses. I want to take the bows."

"Glamour and glory. That's all you're after."

"Exactly." Binky's small face brightened. "I've had to live with you as my brother all my life. I think it's time for some glamour and glory, don't you?"

Egg snorted and opened his mouth to respond, but before he could speak Lexi interrupted: "Egg's right about production. I'd like to work on costuming myself."

"That would be perfect for you, Lexi!" Binky enthused. "You've been sewing your own clothes for years. What a great idea!"

"For Lexi it's okay. For you it would be boring," Egg pointed out.

Binky ignored him. She glanced at her watch. "We'd better get to the gym. Mrs. Waverly will be starting tryouts soon."

When Jennifer, Lexi, Egg and Binky walked into the gymnasium, they saw it was surprisingly full of would-be actors and actresses.

Lexi breathed a sigh of relief when she spotted Peggy's slim form on the far side of the gym. "She did show up for tryouts," Lexi whispered to Jennifer.

"Great. This will be good for her. I hope she gets a part."

Mrs. Waverly stood at a podium on stage. "People! People! May I have your attention, *please*!" Everyone was milling about, too excited to pay attention. Mrs. Waverly looked harried. Her blond hair was stacked high on her head and tipped slightly to the right. Two yellow number-two pencils stuck out of the curls. She clapped her hands. "Attention, please! We need to get organized."

Gradually the students turned toward the stage. Mrs. Waverly lifted a stack of play books from beneath the podium and handed them to two students who stood at her right. "We will be handing out copies of the play for you to look over. I know some of you have already done so and chosen the part you'd like to audition for. I'll choose the passage I'd like to hear. I assume most of you are familiar with *Macbeth* . . ." Mrs. Waverly paused as she looked over the crowd of doubtful expressions.

" . . . but for those who aren't, I'll summarize the story."

"Oh, good," Binky whispered to Lexi. "I tried to read it and couldn't make any sense of it."

Lexi covered a grin. Binky was awfully confident about becoming a star in *Macbeth*, considering she didn't understand the play.

"Macbeth and Banquo are two warriors in eleventh-century Scotland," Mrs. Waverly began. "On their way home from battle, they meet three witches on a lonely heath. The three greet Macbeth as 'Thane of Glamis, Thane of Cawdor, and King Hereafter.' At that point in time, Macbeth was only Thane of Glamis."

Mrs. Waverly gave the confused audience a weak smile. "To help you understand the importance of the position, a *thane* was something like a governor.

"When Macbeth returns to his home, he discovers that one of the witches' prophesies has come true. He has been named Thane of Cawdor! It occurs to Macbeth that someday he might actually be *king*.

"The seed for a wicked idea has been planted: if Macbeth kills the current king, he will become the new king. Lady Macbeth encourages her husband to commit this dastardly deed. When it is carried out, Macbeth is crowned successor to the throne."

"Heavy-duty stuff," Egg muttered.

"This murder leads to a series of others, so Macbeth returns to the witches on the heath to demand more prophecies. They show Macbeth a series of images that include a bodyless head warning Macbeth against Macduff, and a blood-covered child who says, 'None of woman born shall harm Macbeth.' A third prophecy indicates that Macbeth will be safe until 'Birnam Wood comes to Dunsinane.'

"Meanwhile, Lady Macbeth begins to walk in her sleep. The crimes that she and her husband have committed drive her to madness. She ultimately commits suicide. Her husband dies at the hand of Macduff, the warrior who had sworn to kill Macbeth with his own sword."

"Oh-h-h-h, how gross!" Binky wrinkled her nose. "What a gory story."

"This is a different type of play from others we've attempted at Cedar River," Mrs. Waverly continued. "It is rather dark and somber. But *Macbeth* is one of the best-loved plays in the world today. I think you students are ready to tackle something more difficult than plays we've done in the past. The beauty and melodic poetry of Shakespeare can be best understood when spoken aloud. Those of you who decide to take part in this play will come away with a new appreciation for this great writer and his work."

Minda, Tressa, and Gina sauntered by Lexi and Jennifer. Minda brushed her blond hair away from her collar with a dramatic flick of her hand. "I don't know why anyone else is bothering to try out for Lady Macbeth," she said cockily.

"You're a shoe-in for Lady M," Tressa assured her.

"What a great part for you," Gina gushed.

Binky poked Egg in the ribs. "Why don't you try out for Macbeth? I'd love to see you and Minda acting together."

Egg grimaced. "Now I know for sure I'm going to sign up to work on lights. I wouldn't be on that stage for anything. Not with Minda Hannaford parading around with murder on her mind!"

Chapter Three

If Binky squirmed anymore, she'd fall out of her chair. Lexi had watched her friend wiggle and fuss through the entire first period of the day.

"I just can't concentrate!" Binky leaned so far out of her chair the desk nearly toppled.

Lexi was thankful for the class bell. Binky bounced to her feet like a gigantic jack-in-the-box and followed Lexi into the hallway.

"What can be taking Mrs. Waverly so long? I thought she'd have the play cast posted before first hour."

"Maybe you were all so good that she couldn't make up her mind," Lexi suggested cheerfully. "She's probably having a terrible time deciding who should play Lady Macbeth, you or Minda."

"That shouldn't be difficult. There's only one person who's truly right for that part." She struck one of her star-like poses and Lexi burst out laughing.

"Oh, Binky, you're too much."

"Mr. Raddis is going to be a great co-director. He knows so much about history. He's the perfect person to keep the play authentic." Binky didn't have to add that Mr. Raddis was one of her favorite teachers. "It's

too bad that Mr. Raddis isn't casting the play. I'd be
Lady Macbeth for sure."

Lexi had the fleeting thought that Binky Mc-
Naughton would make the tiniest, bounciest, young-
est-looking Lady Macbeth in all of theater history.
But Lexi's thoughts returned to other concerns.

"Where was Peggy last hour, Binky?"

"I didn't see her. I've had my mind on something
else." Binky waved the play book in Lexi's face.
"Shakespeare can occupy a lot of one's brain cells,
you know."

"It's not like Peggy to miss school," Lexi persisted. Even when things were really sour in her life,
Peggy never missed classes.

In the hallway, Lexi ran into Jennifer. "Have you
seen Peggy? She missed first-hour class. Where could
she be?"

"She's right there."

Lexi spun around to see Peggy walking out of the
administration offices. She carried a bright yellow
excuse slip in her hand.

"See, Lexi? You didn't have to worry . . ." Binky's
voice trailed away. "What's *wrong* with her?"

Peggy was limping. She winced each time she
lifted her right foot, as if in pain.

Jennifer moved quickly to her side. "Do you need
some help? Do you want to sit down?" Lexi and Binky
hovered nearby.

Peggy waved her hand in the air. "It's nothing.
Really."

"It doesn't look like *nothing* to me," Jennifer said
pointedly. "What happened?"

"Everybody is making too much of this," Peggy

said with a forced smile. "Let go of me, Jennifer, or you're going to be late for your next class. *You* don't have an excuse for it."

The warning bell sounded. "Go on," Peggy insisted. "We'll talk about it later."

Reluctantly, the three left Peggy standing in the hallway. Lexi turned again to catch the pained expression on Peggy's face.

The rest of the morning Lexi was consumed with thoughts of Peggy and what could have caused her limp. She was more than eager to get to the cafeteria at noon to hear her friend's explanation.

———

"If we have this disgusting food again, I'm going to croak." Jennifer dawdled her spoon through the concoction on her plate.

"I think it's refried beans," Egg said, eating them like he was starved. "They're not bad if you don't stop to look at them. Mix them with the rice."

"Refried beans—yuck!" Jennifer gingerly placed a napkin over her plate.

"Are you finished already?" a male voice inquired.

Lexi noticed the pink blush rise in Jennifer's cheeks. "No. Not exactly. I'm just covering the mess so it doesn't revolt me. Want to join us?" Her voice was hopeful.

"Sit down, Matthew, my man," Egg said with an expansive wave. "I'm beginning to feel outnumbered with all these women around. I wish Todd would hurry up and get back to school."

Matt Windsor slid onto the bench across from

Egg. "That doesn't sound like a bad problem. You're the envy of all the guys in school." Matt gave Jennifer, Binky, and Lexi a wide smile.

"Save it for someone who believes you, Matt," Binky said cheerfully. "It's *your* charm that's irresistible."

As Lexi listened to the banter, she thought about all the ways Matt Windsor had changed since she'd first met him.

When Lexi moved to Cedar River, she thought of Matt as a dangerous character. He had a sullen look, and wore his black hair in a dramatic cut to match the ring in his ear. His eyes looked like flat, black stones—completely expressionless.

Now his hair was more conservative, and he had a smile on his face. He looked nothing like the brooding boy he'd been.

He had much to overcome in his life. His father and stepmother's troubled marriage had nearly forced him out of his own home. Matt had softened considerably since then. His smile was bright and open and his dark eyes twinkled mischievously.

Lexi glanced at Jennifer. She'd been a loyal friend to Matt through the bad times and the good. Lexi had the feeling their relationship was about to be "on again."

"So, what's new, everyone?" Matt said, opening a carton of milk.

"The play is the biggest news," Lexi said. "How did the tryouts go for you?"

Matt blushed a little. "I don't know. Mrs. Waverly just said 'Good job' when I finished reading. She says that to everyone. For some reason, I like Shakespeare. Particularly *Macbeth*."

"Do you think you'll get a big part?" Egg asked.

"It's doubtful," Matt responded. "It would be all right to be Banquo or Macduff, though."

"Minda thinks she's going to be Lady Macbeth," Binky stated flatly. She raised her pert little nose into the air. "She just doesn't know what kind of competition she has."

"Does that mean you're shooting for the part of Lady Macbeth, Binky?"

"She thinks it's her chance to become a star," Egg spoke before she could answer. "My sister has some weird ideas."

"Don't discourage her, Egg. She might be a great Lady Macbeth. Who knows? She could bring an entirely new interpretation to the role."

"I didn't know you were so interested in the theater, Matt," Lexi said.

Matt blushed, something that was easy for him, now that he'd shed his tough-guy image.

"When I was younger, and my parents were fighting, I'd sneak out of the house and go to the community theater playhouse a few blocks away. I'd sit in the dark and listen to the actors rehearse their lines. I'd get lost in it and forget all about the trouble at home."

Now Matt blushed flame-red. "It probably sounds goofy, but I really do like the theater."

Lexi was pondering Matt's words when Binky interrupted her train of thought: "Wasn't Peggy going to join us for lunch today? We're almost done and she's not here yet."

Lexi turned in time to see Peggy join the dwindling cafeteria line.

"What's wrong with her?" Matt's dark eyes were riveted on Peggy's limping form. "She looks terrible. Did she fall off a bike, have a car accident or what?"

"It's a big mystery to us," Jennifer said frankly. "We'll have to ask her."

It was obviously painful for her to put her full weight down on one foot, but Peggy gamely made her way across the newly waxed floor.

"What happened?"

"Just call me Hopalong." Peggy placed her tray on the table and patted her bad leg. "I had to wait till the noon rush was over so I could walk down the hall without getting knocked over. If I'd fallen and someone stepped on my head, I'd really be in bad shape, wouldn't I?" She tapped her skull, "Of course, there's not much up there to damage."

Lexi wasn't accustomed to hearing Peggy make jokes, especially about herself. It had been months since Peggy had acted so comical.

"All kidding aside, Peggy, what happened to you?" Egg stared intently at Peggy's leg.

She grimaced as she sat down.

"Whatever it is, it looks like it hurts," Matt said.

"Oh, it's nothing. Just something really stupid."

"Accidents are usually stupid, Peggy," Lexi said. "What happened?"

It was obvious to Lexi from Peggy's expression that she didn't want to say what happened.

"Something really silly. I feel dumb talking about it."

"That doesn't matter. Tell us," Binky commanded.

"It wouldn't have happened if I didn't have such a big appetite."

"Huh?" Egg wore a blank expression. "I have a great appetite."

"I couldn't go to sleep last night because I was hungry. I must have lain in bed almost an hour trying to convince myself that I didn't need a bowl of ice cream. The longer I lay there, the hungrier I got. Finally, about midnight, I decided to go downstairs and find something to eat. I guess I should have stayed in bed," Peggy said ruefully. "As I was going down the stairs, I tripped on the hem of my robe and fell."

"Ouch!" Binky blurted.

"I made a terrible clatter, woke my parents, and nearly scared my mother out of her wits. I can't believe I did anything so stupid. I'm so clumsy.

"Anyway, I was sure I hadn't broken anything, but this morning, when I got up, I had a really bad bruise on my leg. My mother made me go to the clinic and have my leg X-rayed. That's why I was late for school."

"What did the doctor say?" Binky loved a story with drama.

"He said my leg was only bruised. It'll be stiff and sore and I'll limp for a while, but that's all."

"I'm sorry, Peggy," Jennifer said. "But I'm glad it wasn't any worse."

"Me too," Peggy admitted. "But I still feel dumb about being so clumsy."

Binky, who always said whatever came to her mind, crossed her thin arms over her chest and looked at Peggy with a puzzled expression. "I'm really surprised you did that, Peggy."

"Well, it was hardly her choice," Egg pointed out.

"But, Peggy, you're so athletic and graceful on the basketball court," Binky went on. "It seems weird that you'd stumble on the stairs. Besides, I thought your bathrobe was short, not long. How could you trip on the hem?"

Peggy blushed deeply. "I don't want to talk about it anymore," she said sternly. "I've had to explain this limp to practically every person I've met today. So, if you don't mind . . ."

It was a clear-cut end to the conversation. But instead of resolving anything for Lexi, it made her more curious. Binky was right, Peggy *did* have a short bathrobe, not a long one. How *had* she managed to trip and injure herself so badly?

Chapter Four

Egg was standing near Lexi's classroom door when she and Binky emerged.

"Hurry up. I've been waiting for you."

"What for?"

"I want to see if the play cast has been posted."

"Can't you go see for yourself?"

"I volunteered for lighting," Egg reminded Binky. "You and Jennifer were the ones who went through tryouts."

Lexi was relieved that she'd volunteered to help with the costuming. She didn't envy the nervous expression on Binky's face at this moment.

"Where *is* Jennifer?"

"She couldn't wait. She's already on her way to the bulletin board. Come on." Egg towed them through the hallways.

"You're more eager than I am to find out about this," Binky muttered.

"Are you having second thoughts?"

"The play is going to be a lot of work and a lot of extra hours. It'll cut a real hole in my study time."

Egg snorted. "You spend every evening *looking* for things to cut holes in your study time, Binky. This is the perfect answer."

There was a crowd gathered around the bulletin board. Everyone was hooting with laughter. Some boys were clutching their sides, laughing as though they'd just heard the funniest joke ever.

"That's weird," Binky commented. "What's so humorous about the cast for *Macbeth*?"

Just then Minda Hannaford broke away from the crowd. Her face was red and contorted. When Tim Anders got in her way, she gave him a shove so hard that he went skittering into a bank of lockers. Minda stomped away in a fury.

"What's her problem?"

"I'll bet she didn't get a part." A satisfied expression settled over Binky's face.

The conversation of the students echoed Binky's prediction.

"Serves her right. That's all I can say."

"Perfect casting, don't you think?"

"I didn't think Mrs. Waverly would dare . . ."

Egg, Lexi, and Binky pushed their way to the front of the crowd where Jennifer stood. Her eyes were riveted on the typed sheet tacked to the board.

"Minda didn't get a part," Binky said with mild elation.

Jennifer turned to stare at her. "What makes you say that? Of course Minda got a part."

"She did?" Binky's shoulders sagged. "I was sure she hadn't gotten Lady Macbeth. I suppose that means I'm out of luck."

"Minda didn't get Lady Macbeth." Jennifer pointed to the list. "She's one of the witches."

Egg emitted a hoot. "Minda? A witch? Perfecto!

Yes!" He punched the air over his head. "Primo casting if I've ever seen it."

Binky made a weak sound in her throat as she stared at the list. "But Egg, *I'm* one of the witches, too."

Egg's arm fell to his side. "Oh. Uh. Sorry about that. Congratulations, Binky! You'll be a super . . ." He tried to hide a grin. ". . . witch."

"Don't look so unhappy, Binky." Jennifer's eyes were shining. "I'm the third witch. It's perfect, don't you see? What a great part."

"You *want* to be a witch?" Binky muttered in disbelief. "But they're ugly old hags!"

"They're also the best parts in the play." Jennifer's eyes gleamed. "Double, double, toil and trouble, caldron boil and caldron bubble." She made a stirring motion with her hands. "It's going to be great fun. The witches are meaty parts that you can really sink your teeth into; really gives you a chance to act."

"We certainly got three separate reactions from the witches, didn't we? We have a happy witch, a doubtful witch, and one who looks like she's about to murder someone.

"Oh well," Lexi said thoughtfully, "I suppose a person brings his own personality to the stage. How about you, Egg? Are you in lighting?"

"You bet! Exactly where I wanted to be. This is going to be great. I've already got some ideas about how to make Binky and Minda look really scary."

Binky gave another weak little groan. "Ooooh, I don't think I'm going to like this."

"Lexi! Did you know you're head costume designer?"

"I am?" Lexi peered over Egg's shoulder. "I'd almost forgotten to look for my name. Good. It'll be fun. I can do what I love to do and still take part in the play."

"We're all happy, then," Jennifer said cheerfully. "Except for Minda." She glanced at Binky. "You'll be happy soon. I guarantee it."

"I doubt I'll ever be happy again. A *witch*. Mrs. Waverly thinks I look like a witch."

"No, Binky," Lexi said. "It only proves what a good actress you are. It doesn't mean she thinks you *look* like a witch."

"She does. I know she does. This is the most depressing day of my life. How am I ever going to be discovered as an actress if I'm hidden in ugly witch's clothing?"

"If you're a good actress, it will shine through," Lexi assured her. "Besides, I don't think there will be any Hollywood agents scouting at our school play, Binky. Think of this as experience. Paying your dues."

"A witch. Mrs. Waverly thought I looked like a witch."

"Just ignore her," Egg advised. "She'll get over it. She always does." He snapped his fingers. "Hey! We've been so worried about Binky and Minda, we didn't even notice who got the part of Macbeth—or Lady Macbeth."

They all turned again to the cast listing.

"Well, what do you know about that?" Egg sounded amazed. "Matt Windsor is Macbeth."

The announcement brought a smile to Lexi's face. "Good for Matt. It will be exciting for him. All the hours in that theater as a child have paid off."

Egg ran his finger down the list. "Jerry Randall is Banquo. He's ambitious—working at the Hamburger Shack and being in the play. Brian James, from church, is Macduff. The part of Malcolm is to be played by Tim Anders."

The characters of Donalbain, Lennox, Ross, Old and Young Siward were given to boys Lexi didn't know well. Still, a surprising number of her friends had made it into the cast. She was already anticipating the fun.

"Look who's going to be Lady Macbeth!" Egg's finger rested on the last name on the list. They all stared.

"Peggy Madison!" Binky squeaked.

"Yeah? What's up?" Peggy sauntered toward the group. "Did I hear someone call my name?"

"You! You! You're Peggy Madison!" Binky stammered.

"Yes, I am."

"No! Don't you get it?" Binky pointed to the cast list then to Peggy and back again.

"What is she talking about?"

"She's starstruck, Peggy. She's never been in the presence of a real Shakespearean actress before," Egg explained.

"What are you talking about?" Peggy glanced casually at the cast list. Everyone watched as her eyes ran down the list of characters. "Me? Lady Macbeth? I got the part?"

"Congratulations!"

"Good going, Peggy."

"You'll be great."

She accepted the congratulations, but her expression was pained. It was as though she'd received a gift she wasn't sure she wanted.

"Let's go to the Hamburger Shack and celebrate," Egg suggested. "It's not every day that we have Lady Macbeth in our midst."

Peggy said grimly, "I hope I didn't make a mistake by trying out."

"No mistake. You'll be great," Binky assured her. "If I couldn't have the part, you're the next best choice."

"Thanks, Binky. I'm glad you feel that way."

Egg glanced at his watch. "I have to be home early tonight, so let's go now. Peggy, may I escort you?" He gallantly held out his arm.

Peggy patted his cheek. "You go ahead, I'll catch up with you in a few minutes." She turned toward the girl's restroom. "I have to make a stop first."

"I'll wait for you," Lexi offered. "I don't mind. They can go on ahead and get a booth."

"No, really. You go too," Peggy said quickly. "I don't want to hold you up."

"Hold us up? Peggy, you're the one we're celebrating!"

"Go ahead without me," Peggy said firmly. "I'll be along in a few minutes. I need to be alone. Don't worry about me, Lexi, please."

Now what was wrong with Peggy? She should have been delighted to be chosen for such an important part in the play. Instead, it seemed she was trying to keep her unhappiness in check.

And what was this nonsense about needing to be alone in the restroom? Lexi wondered. The last thing

any of them wanted from Peggy was more weird behavior.

Egg, Binky, Jennifer, and Lexi arrived at the
Hamburger Shack in time to claim the last booth.
Jerry Randall was cleaning the table off when they
arrived.

"Congratulations!" Egg slapped Jerry on the
back. "I hear you're going to be a star."

"Did Mrs. Waverly post the play cast?"

"You mean you haven't heard yet? You got the
part of Banquo."

"I did? Great! My aunt and uncle have been nag-
ging at me to do something other than work at the
Shack. This should satisfy them."

"How do *you* feel about it, Jerry?" Lexi asked.

He considered her question for a moment.
"Happy. Excited, I guess. It'll be nice to do something
different for a change. Who's playing Macbeth?"

"Matt Windsor. And Peggy Madison is going to
be Lady Macbeth."

Jerry's eyebrows arched. "No kidding? They
should be great together."

"And," Egg continued in a dramatic voice, "we
have another star in our midst."

"Oh, quit goofing off," Binky socked him in the
chest.

"Ooof," Egg grunted. "I'd like you to meet Cedar
River High's greatest witch, Binky McNaughton."

A slow grin spread across Jerry's face. "You're one
of the three witches? Congratulations!"

"What about me?" Jennifer interrupted. "I'm a witch, too."

"We just think you're so much more like a witch, we tend to forget about it," Egg said.

Jennifer glared at Egg and poked him in the ribs.

"But, the best part of all," he continued when he could breathe again, "is the third witch. Have you got any guesses?"

"I don't know," Jerry laughed. "I haven't got a clue. Who's the third witch?"

"Minda Hannaford!"

Jerry's jaw dropped. "Minda? A witch? How did they get her to settle for that?"

"I don't think Minda had any choice. She went storming off, furious. I have a hunch Mrs. Waverly's getting an earful right now."

"I think Minda might make a good witch. She certainly has the personality for it."

"Oh, Jerry, she's not that bad," Lexi came to Minda's defense. "Sometimes she's just a little . . . difficult . . . that's all." She slid into the booth. "We need to order, Jerry. I'm starved."

When Peggy finally arrived, she seemed more relaxed than she had at school. The tension was gone from her face, replaced by an unfamiliar laxness about her features. Instead of being uptight, she tossed her head and smiled as if she hadn't a care in the world. Lexi was startled by the change.

As Peggy slid into the booth, the overwhelming aroma of strong perfume came with her. Jennifer coughed indiscreetly, and Egg's face screwed up in a frown. "What's that smell?"

"How does it feel to be Lady Macbeth?" Lexi

asked, interrupting Egg's question to save Peggy from embarrassment. "Are you excited?"

"Surprised mostly," Peggy admitted. "I was sure Minda Hannaford would get the part."

"Minda thought so, too," Binky said. "I guess it serves her right. It's worth being a witch to see Minda taken down a notch or two."

Peggy broke into gales of high-pitched laughter.

"Oh, Binky, you are *soooo* cute," Peggy gushed, drawing Binky's cheeks between the palms of her hands. "Isn't she cute?" Peggy turned to Jennifer and Lexi, still clutching Binky's face.

Lexi and Jennifer exchanged glances. What was Peggy doing that for? And why had she doused on so much perfume before coming here?

Peggy released Binky and stared into the bottom of her beverage glass, giggling to herself.

"Want to tell us what's so funny?" Egg asked. "So we can laugh, too?"

Peggy threw her head back in a carefree fashion. "I was thinking about Minda. I'll bet she's green with envy right now. Can you believe it? I beat Minda Hannaford out of a part!"

It was not like Peggy to gloat. Everything about her since she'd come from the school seemed odd. There was a giddy silliness about her that Lexi hadn't noticed before. Something had happened to Peggy between the time they'd left her at the high school and when she'd arrived at the Hamburger Shack.

Peggy drew a small atomizer of perfume from her purse. "I just got this at the mall yesterday, and it smells great! Want to try some?" Peggy began to spray it around, laughing with glee.

"*More* perfume? Ugh!" Egg yelped, ducking under the table.

Lexi watched, growing more perplexed by the moment. Why was Peggy's personality taking such a roller coaster ride from depressed to silly and back again? They'd seen it happen in a matter of minutes. It was as if Peggy were a different person!

Chapter Five

Lexi's step quickened as she neared Todd's room at the rehabilitation hospital. She hadn't seen him for two days and was eager to discuss with him all that had happened.

"Hi, stranger." Todd was sitting in a chair surrounded by pillows. His dark blond hair was neatly combed, and he wore sweatpants and a T-shirt that enhanced the blue of his eyes.

"Hi, yourself. How are you doing?"

"The physical therapists tell me I'm their best patient. Handsome, charming, and good-natured."

Lexi laughed. "How about your exercises?"

"Oh, those." Todd waved his hand. "Who needs to be good at that when you're the best patient?"

"Very funny. Now tell me the truth."

"I can't fool you for a minute, can I? I'm really doing fine. Ahead of schedule, actually." He gave a little grimace. "That doesn't mean *I* think it's going fast enough, of course. I've been doing a lot of complaining about old Betsy here." Todd tapped the walker standing next to him.

"You're ungrateful, if you ask me." Lexi seated herself in the chair across from him. "That walker has taken you many miles."

"Right. Up and down hospital corridors. Hand me those crutches, Lexi. I want to show you something."

Lexi reached for the crutches leaning against the far wall. "I don't know if I should give you these," she teased. "If I say something you don't like, you can poke me with them."

"Then don't say anything that I won't like."

It took Todd a moment to maneuver the crutches into place. He settled the rubber tips in front of the legs of his chair. With strong hands he gripped the handles, and painstakingly raised himself to a standing position. Then he slid the arm rests under his armpits and settled his weight down. He rocked and swayed unsteadily for a moment until he got his balance. Then, slowly, he began to walk.

A sheen of sweat broke out on his forehead, but the determined expression on his face never faltered. Slow step after slow step, Todd walked across the room. When he neared his bed, he sat down on the edge and allowed the crutches to clatter to the floor. It didn't matter that he had only gone a few steps, or that he'd been too weary to make it into the hallway. Nothing mattered except the fact that Todd was walking. Lexi's tears showed her joy and relief.

"You're supposed to be laughing, or at least smiling," Todd pointed out. "What's with the tears?"

"You really *are* going to be okay, aren't you?"

"Sure I am. Wasn't that proof enough? I'm waiting for the day when I'll be able to throw the crutches away too."

Until this moment, Lexi'd had seeds of doubt about Todd's recovery, despite what his parents, the doctors, and even Todd had said. In the back of her mind she'd always worried that he would never leave the wheelchair. Now she felt confident that Todd really would be completely well again.

"You didn't believe I'd ever do it, did you, Lexi?" he said softly.

"I didn't know how much I'd doubted it until just now."

"I'm surprised at you, Lexi. I thought you were the one with all the faith. As it turns out, I have some faith of my own. I *know* I'm going to make it. It might take time, but it'll happen." Todd's eyes were clear and shining.

"God's helping me, Lexi. I couldn't do any of this on my own. There are mornings in therapy when I'm so tired I want to bawl like a baby. Just when I think I can't do one more thing, the therapists introduce another exercise that I have to do before I can go to my room."

"Oh, Todd . . ."

"It's times like those when I hear a voice in the back of my brain saying, 'Come on, Todd, you can do it. I've got plans for you. They don't include being in a wheelchair. One more step. One more exercise. One more hour."

It was awesome to see God at work in Todd's life. Lexi marveled at what God could do when a person turned every part of his life over to Him.

Todd lifted himself by his forearms and scooted to the top of the bed. "I know walking with crutches may not look like much work to you, Lexi, but it's like taking part in a triathalon for me. I've turned into a wimp, haven't I?"

"The exact opposite," Lexi said indignantly. "You're the *least* wimpy guy I know." She giggled.

"What's so funny?"

"I just had this vision of men in short dresses and colored tights."

"Huh? Are you losing your mind?"

"Not at all. I'm the head of costume design for *Macbeth*."

"And you're going to put all the guys in tights and tunics?"

"It's a thought, but I might have a mutiny on my hands. Do you think the guys would do it? Matt Windsor is Macbeth. Brian James is Macduff. Jerry Randall got the part of Banquo. There are several other guys, of course, but I don't know them."

"Matt strutting around on the stage in tights?" Todd thought about it for a moment. "It doesn't sound very likely, but you never know about Matt. He's a pretty complex character. He might not mind, if it fits the part."

"That's exactly what I thought. Matt told us a story about how as a child he used to escape to the back row of a community theater to watch the rehearsals. I think Matt will be the least of my problems."

"How about Egg? He wouldn't wear tights, would he?"

"Egg's doing the lighting."

"You're safe there then."

"Guess what! Peggy got the part of Lady Macbeth."

"Really? She'll be very good. Peggy needs to do

something significant to get her mind off the last few months."

"That's for sure." Lexi told Todd about Peggy's strange behavior at the Hamburger Shack. "She's unpredictable, really. Gloomy and depressed one minute; giddy and silly the next. Her highs are high and her lows are frightening. There must be an explanation for it, but I can't figure it out." The furrows in Lexi's forehead deepened. "If I didn't know better, I'd think Peggy was on something."

"You mean drugs?"

"I haven't had much experience around people who've used them, so I couldn't say for sure."

"Alcohol?" Todd knew more about these things than Lexi.

"I don't know much about that either, frankly."

"Just watch her closely," Todd advised.

"I've been trying, but she's pretty elusive. She's become secretive lately. She fell down the steps and got a huge bruise on her leg. She said she came downstairs in the night to look for something to eat and tripped on the hem of her robe."

"What's so strange about that?" Todd asked.

"Nothing, except that Peggy doesn't have a long robe. I can't imagine why she'd lie."

"You sound awfully suspicious, Lexi. I don't understand."

"I don't either," Lexi admitted. "I just worry about Peggy's strange behavior. The fall is just one more thing to think about."

"Peggy's been through a lot. She gave up her baby, and then Chad committed suicide. That's enough to change anyone."

"I know. I know. But neither of those things seem to be the problem right now. I don't know how to explain it, Todd, but Peggy's just . . . different. She wanted to brush off the fall she had like it was nothing at all."

"I hope she wasn't hurt more than she's willing to admit." Todd was especially compassionate and sensitive about injuries, now that he'd become aware of his own limitations. "Are you sure you're not just reading too much into things?"

"Maybe I'm looking for another mystery to solve, like the time Holly Agnew was kidnapped. Do you think that's my problem?"

"I'd be more apt to say your problem is an overactive imagination, Lexi."

"My father blames me for that regularly."

"I'm glad Peggy got the part of Lady Macbeth. Maybe this play will be a turning point in her life."

"If anyone deserves the part, she does," Lexi agreed. "I think a lot of people have high hopes for this play." Lexi's eyes began to gleam. "There's some other big news I haven't told you yet. Mrs. Waverly did some very *creative* casting."

"How creative?"

"Well," Lexi began mischievously, "do you want to take a guess at who the three witches are?"

"No way." He shook his head firmly. "That's like asking me to guess how much a girl weighs. No matter what I guess, I'll end up in trouble."

"Let's just say that our friend Binky was not too happy about being chosen."

"Binky? One of the witches?"

"She wanted to be Lady Macbeth. She thought

her big competition was going to be Minda."

"If Minda isn't Lady Macbeth, who is she?" There was a brief silence, and then Todd read the expression on Lexi's face. "You're kidding me, right? Minda? One of the three witches?" Suddenly he began to laugh. "Minda, a witch?" He laughed until tears came to his eyes.

"If Minda and Binky are two of the witches, who's the third? Jennifer?"

Lexi snapped her fingers. "Right on!"

"Now I've heard everything!"

"Jennifer's excited. She thinks it's the best part in the play."

"In other words, she's going to ham it up and *make* it the best part."

"You've got that right."

"Binky and Minda will have their jobs cut out for them keeping up with her."

"Jennifer's even more excited about being at rehearsals with Matt. They're getting along again—as of this week."

Todd smiled. "What did Minda say when she heard she got the part of a witch?"

"I haven't talked to her since the list went up. But the way she stormed away from the bulletin board says she wasn't a happy camper. If Mrs. Waverly had been in her office at the time, we might have heard the explosion for miles. But Minda seems to be calming down again."

Todd's expression grew wistful. "I wish I could be in the play."

Lexi could see his frustration. "Oh, Todd . . ."

Then he snapped out of it. "But I'm going to walk

again, Lexi. That's the big thing right now. I have a lot to be thankful for."

"There'll be a part for you next year, I'm sure of it." Lexi blushed a little. "I hope it's a good play, because I really want to be in it with you."

"Lexi—is that why you didn't try out this time?"

"Partly. But I love to sew, and I've always wanted to be a costume designer. I think it's a good idea to do what I do best."

"Next year, Lexi. We'll be in the play together and we'll have a great time." Todd closed his eyes wearily.

Lexi hurt with him. She could sympathize with the frustration he was feeling, and the isolation from his friends. But right now, his best and most important performance was here in the hospital—for the therapists and doctors.

"I'm going to church on Sunday," Todd changed the subject. "There's a specially equipped van that takes the rehab patients out shopping, to church, to an occasional movie. And Pastor Lake has been coming to visit me regularly. He's been an important part of my healing process.

"I've had so much support through all of this, Lexi. It's been hard, but there have been some good times and good people. You're one of them; Pastor Lake is another. God's enabled me through all of you to survive this. I must admit, though, it's going to be hard to sit in the audience and watch all my friends perform Shakespeare."

"Everyone's getting a little worried. They all claim they can't *understand* Shakespeare, much less *perform* it. But Mr. Raddis and Mrs. Waverly tell us the cast will become real Shakespeare fans before they're finished."

"Even Minda?"

"That's a little hard to imagine, but who knows?"

After a few minutes Lexi glanced at her watch. "I've got to go. I promised Ben I'd help him with an art project tonight."

"How is Ben? I miss that guy."

"He misses you, too. There's an art show at the Academy. Ben wondered if he could come up with something special that would make you happy."

"Me? He's a great kid, Lexi. Almost as great as his sister." He reached out and took Lexi's hand. He squeezed the tips of her fingers gently. "Thanks, Lex."

As she descended the hospital steps into the night air, Lexi was happier than she'd been in a long, long time.

Chapter Six

"Aren't you excited?" Binky jogged beside Lexi and Jennifer as they walked toward the school gymnasium. Her hair flew in ten directions and her eyes sparkled. "This is going to be fun. I don't even mind the fact that I'm going to be a witch."

"I've been reading the play. Jennifer's right," Lexi commented. "The witches *do* have the best parts. They'll be the most intriguing to watch."

Jennifer nodded vigorously in agreement. "Have you got any good costuming ideas for us yet, Lexi?"

"Black isn't my best color," Binky interrupted. "Do witches always have to wear black? Maybe gray silk would do. How does that sound? Something long and flowy. Yes, gray is definitely more my color . . ." Binky babbled on.

Tonight would be the first rehearsal, and there was an undeniable energy in the air.

Minda was just inside the school doorway, dressed in a white denim outfit with a bright blue shirt and matching earrings. Her blond ponytail was stacked high on her head, and her makeup was flawless.

The boy who'd been assigned to play Ross, a cousin of Macduff, sauntered by. "Trying to prove to everyone you're not really a witch, Minda?" he teased.

Minda shot him a withering glance.

"Did you see the look she gave him?" Binky whispered. "She's *perfect* for the part. I can't think of anyone who could play a witch better than Minda."

"Of course, she's got the advantage. She comes by it naturally. But you and I are pretty good actresses, Binky. I'm sure we can keep up."

Lexi still had mixed feelings about Minda. She could be very cruel, but she also had a compassionate side that showed itself at the most surprising times.

Lexi was thankful that she wasn't in a starring role herself. Being costume designer was the perfect job for her. Her clashes with Minda would be few and far between. That was the best part.

In the gymnasium, Mrs. Waverly and Mr. Raddis were on stage attempting to make order of the chaos.

"May I have your attention, please?" Mr. Raddis's voice boomed across the gym. "Macbeth, Lady Macbeth, and the other large speaking parts will be working with me on their lines this evening. Those of you in charge of costuming, publicity, and set construction will work with Mrs. Waverly. We're going to begin blocking on stage immediately. Those of you in production should follow Mrs. Waverly to the Home Economics room where you'll discuss your responsibilities."

Mr. Raddis pointed to Egg. "Edward McNaughton, you're in charge of lighting. Please stay here. You'll need to get a feel for the play right away. I'd like you to listen to these initial rehearsals even though we aren't going to be working through the complete play immediately. Witches, I'd like you in this corner, please."

Minda, Jennifer, and Binky scampered to the spot Mr. Raddis indicated. "Macbeth, if you'd step up here, please." Lazily, Matt Windsor mounted the steps to the top of the stage.

Lexi fell into step with Mrs. Waverly.

"Lexi. There you are. There's no need for you to come with me. I'd rather have you stop in our costume department and begin looking through the clothing. See what ideas you have for wardrobe. I've jotted down a few notes of my own." Mrs. Waverly handed her a sheet of paper. "See what you can come up with. Our costume department is not very extensive, but we always seem to manage to find something that works."

"I can sew anything else we need," Lexi offered. "If the patterns are uncomplicated, I can do them quite quickly."

"That's one of the reasons I'm so delighted you've accepted this job. I have complete faith in your ability, my dear. The door to the costume department is unlocked. Go inside and see what you can find. I'll check with you as soon as I get the others organized."

Lexi disappeared happily into the stuffy room, filled on three sides with clothing racks. Costumes of all description were packed tightly along the walls. The place needed cleaning and organizing. Lexi stood with her hands on her hips staring at the mess.

Maybe if I sorted them by vintage . . . She started at the end of one rack and slowly, examining each piece, separated the costumes into piles. The 1920s went in one stack, a large array of late sixties hippie-garb in another. Lexi set aside three long flowing black dresses of similar design that had possibilities for witches' apparel.

Soon the silence was as oppressive as the mounds of old clothing. Lexi dug out a radio and plugged it into the wall. She could have stayed there for hours, happily imagining how each article could be transformed into something usable on the stage.

She had taken a detour into a box of hats behind the clothing racks when Peggy entered the room. Lexi was seated on the floor, half-buried in the clothing, her legs tucked under her. She might not have noticed Peggy, except for the slight shuffling sound of her footsteps on the rough concrete floor.

Lexi almost said hello, when something in Peggy's manner stopped her. Lexi realized Peggy didn't even see her. And the sound of the radio drowned out the rustling of the hat boxes.

Peggy had obviously entered the room to be alone.

She was supposed to be upstairs with Mr. Raddis becoming acquainted with her lines. Why was she here?

As Lexi watched, Peggy glanced around the room to make sure she was alone. Then she reached into the pocket of her jeans and pulled out a small bottle. It was smaller than a soda bottle, yet larger than a pill bottle. The little flask had fit neatly in Peggy's pocket.

With a twist of her wrist, Peggy broke the seal and lifted the bottle to her lips. Tilting her head back to drink, she closed her eyes, as if to shut out the world. Then Lexi heard Peggy give a gusty sigh and saw her go limp against the wall.

Lexi stared silently, bewildered and alarmed by the unusual scene.

Then, as quickly as she'd come, Peggy left the room. Lexi stood up, her gaze fixed on the doorway through which Peggy had disappeared.

As she stepped to the side of the room where Peggy had been, she noticed a sharp, medicinal odor. It smelled very much like . . . alcohol. That's what it had to be, she decided.

No, I must be imagining things. Lexi tried to deny the thoughts invading her mind. She knew Peggy too well. Some time ago Peggy had professed a profound dislike for alcohol. She wouldn't . . . would she?

"These clothes are going to my brain," Lexi muttered as she draped her arm with a stack of heavy velvet dresses. She would have considered the odd situation further if Mrs. Waverly had not entered at that moment with a yellow pad in hand and three pencils tucked precariously in her hair.

"You've been in here quite awhile, Lexi. Any luck?"

Lexi nodded at the piles of clothes she'd stacked around the room. "Some. I hope you don't mind. I took the liberty to do some organizing."

"Mind? I'm delighted. I've thought it needed to be done, but just never took the time myself to do it."

"I'm sorting, and looking for clothes for the production at the same time. There are several tunics that can be used and a couple of belts. I also found two or three possibilities for the witches' costumes. Something can be worked out with a little creative sewing."

Mrs. Waverly beamed at Lexi. "I knew you were

perfect for this, Lexi, but you're working too hard. Why don't you take a break? Everyone else is about to go home."

"Already?" Lexi glanced at her watch and was startled at the time. "I feel like I've only begun."

"I'll get you some help, Lexi. Two students from the publicity department will be free in a few days."

"It's all right. Actually, I don't mind working alone with the costumes. I spend a lot of my time imagining how they were first used, and how to best showcase them now. I must like the theater better than I first thought."

"Most people do. It gets into your blood. However, I don't expect you to do everything in one night. Come on out for a breath of fresh air."

Lexi followed Mrs. Waverly out of the costume department, across the stage and into the gymnasium. Jennifer and Binky were in the far corner in an animated discussion of their roles as witches.

"How did it go? Is it going to be as much fun as you expected?" Lexi asked.

Jennifer's blue eyes twinkled impishly. "I was born for the part. And Binky was too. We're going to have a lot of fun with it."

"That is, if Minda ever settles down." Binky frowned. "I thought being cast as a witch instead of Lady Macbeth might take her down a notch or two, but that is not the case. She's got all sorts of ideas about how we should portray the parts. She isn't the least bit interested in listening to what Mr. Raddis has to say."

"Wait until she's wearing a fake nose and an artificial wart on her chin!" Jennifer rubbed her hands with glee. "That should give her a new perspective."

Peggy sauntered over to the group. "I'm all finished for the night," she announced. "How about you?"

"Yeah, I guess so." Jennifer held up her play book. "We have some lines to memorize, of course, but we all do."

"Can you all stay overnight? We should be celebrating the beginning of the production. Besides, it's Friday. My mom won't mind if yours don't."

It had been a long time since Peggy Madison had asked any of them to spend the night at her house.

"We could rehearse our lines," Peggy added hopefully. "And make some pizza. How does that sound?"

"Sure, Peggy. Thanks," Lexi said. "Why don't we go call our mothers right now."

Jennifer and Binky nodded.

"If it's okay, just bring your stuff over. I'll go home and make sure we have everything we need for pizza."

"I'll bring a frozen one from home," Lexi offered.

It was good to see Peggy acting so normal again. None of the girls could turn down her invitation.

———

"See you in the morning, Mom." Lexi left for Peggy's house carrying her sleeping bag, the pizza, and a book on the history of costuming. "Bye, Ben."

Ben sat on the front porch, building a wall of blocks. His concentration was so intense he said goodbye without looking up from his task.

Lexi arrived at the Madison home just as Binky and Jennifer did.

"It's a party!" Peggy crowed as she flung open the screen door. "Party, party, party!"

Peggy's attitude changes still puzzled Lexi. How could she be so sullen one moment and giddy the next? When Peggy's mother entered the room, her mood changed again.

"Hello, girls," Mrs. Madison said pleasantly. "How nice to see you. It's been a long time."

Peggy jerked Binky roughly toward the stairway. "Come on, let's get out of here."

"You don't need to be rude, Peggy." Mrs. Madison's voice was calm, but Lexi could see the hurt expression in her eyes.

"These are my friends, Mother, not yours. You don't need to greet them."

"This is my home, too, Peggy," her mother said evenly. Obviously, this was not the first time Peggy and her mother had argued.

"Fine. It's your house, but it's *my* bedroom. We'll go upstairs where we can be *alone*."

"Would you like me to put that pizza in the oven, Lexi?" Mrs. Madison ignored Peggy's glaring expression.

"Why, yes. That would be fine . . ." Lexi was so embarrassed she wanted to cry.

"We'll do it later, Mother. Just *leave us alone*." Peggy took the pizza out of Lexi's hand and tossed it onto the coffee table.

"Your mom's just being nice, Peggy," Binky stammered. "I wouldn't mind having that pizza now."

"She's interfering. This is *my* party. We want to be alone."

Peggy stomped toward the stairway with an

abrupt "Come on." The three girls trailed after her. Lexi looked back to see the sad expression on Mrs. Madison's face.

"What's *wrong* with her?" Binky whispered to Lexi as they mounted the stairs.

Lexi just shook her head.

Peggy's behavior disturbed all of them. Though they tried to act normally as they practiced lines from the play, they felt awkward and uncomfortable.

Later on, feeling tired and anxious to shut out the discomfort, Lexi yawned dramatically. "I don't know about the rest of you, but I'm getting sleepy. I think I'll go to bed. Okay?"

"Me too," Binky answered quickly.

"I'm whipped," Jennifer agreed.

"There was so much excitement today. I think I'll really sleep well tonight," Lexi said.

While Peggy was in the bathroom, Jennifer stormed around the room. "What's gotten into her? I've never seen her like this. She was horrible to her mother."

"I don't know. I don't understand it," Binky said.

"She made her mother cry! Did you see her face?" Jennifer added.

"It's scary. We've got to get to the bottom of this," Lexi said.

All three stared at the door, waiting for Peggy to emerge from the bathroom.

"She's been in there an awfully long time," Binky broke the silence. "What do you think she's doing in there?"

Jennifer snorted mildly. "Probably popping breath mints and gargling mouthwash."

"What do you mean?" Binky asked. Then it dawned on her and her round eyes grew larger. "You don't think Peggy's been drinking, do you?"

"Who knows? She's certainly not acting normal," Jennifer answered. "Haven't you noticed how she sprays perfume on so often? She's probably trying to hide something—like alcohol on her breath."

Lexi bit the inside of her lip. It took all her will power not to mention the scene she'd witnessed in the costume department. Lexi hoped against her better judgment that Peggy was not doing what was becoming more and more obvious to all of them.

"Something is definitely wrong," Binky announced. They'd given up speaking softly.

The bathroom door remained closed. None of the girls wanted to be the one to confront their friend.

Chapter Seven

The upcoming Sunday evening activities eclipsed even Peggy's odd behavior. After church, Binky, Egg, and Lexi met on the freshly mowed grass outside, and watched a group of small boys doing cartwheels and somersaults across the lawn.

"You're going to the youth group tonight, aren't you, Lexi?" Egg asked.

"Of course she is," Binky answered for her. "She wouldn't miss it for anything. I wonder what the program is going to be tonight. Pastor Lake was very mysterious when I asked him."

"He's always got something up his sleeve," Egg said. "I asked him if there was anything I could do to help. He just smiled and said, 'No, but I have something very special planned.'"

"When Pastor Lake says he has something special planned, it's usually great. Remember the 'Search for Christians' party?" Lexi asked.

"You don't think he's organizing something like that do you?" Binky's mouth gaped as she recalled the night they spent creeping across a dark field trying to reach home base without being captured by the opposing team.

"I doubt it." Egg looked serious. "Pastor Lake said tonight's topic was something every teenager needed to know."

"Oh no!" Binky made a face. "It sounds like he's going to lecture us. I can do without that. I get plenty of lectures at home."

"Maybe he keeps us in suspense to make sure we all come," Lexi said.

"If that's what he's doing, the topic is bound to be boring," Binky concluded.

"I guess we'll just have to come tonight and find out," Egg decided.

The church basement was full when Jennifer, Peggy, and Lexi arrived.

"This group has really become popular, hasn't it?" Peggy stared at the crowd.

"Ever since Pastor Lake arrived, things have been happening," Lexi agreed. "Look, there's Minda and some of the Hi-Fives."

"It's amazing that they come," Peggy commented. "And they're not as obnoxious in church as they are in school."

"I'm glad they come," Lexi said. "Maybe they'll take to heart some of what Pastor Lake says."

Jennifer looked at her doubtfully, but did not comment.

Lexi sank into a nearby chair. "The hardest thing about coming to youth group is not having Todd here. I really miss him."

"Yeah. It's tough," Peggy agreed. "I wonder how long he'll have to stay in that rehab hospital?"

"It won't be long now," Lexi said happily. "The doctors are saying he'll be released soon. He'll be able to go out whenever he feels up to it. No more passes."

"Or whenever someone can drive him. Do you think he'll be strong enough to go on his own?"

"He's lifting weights," Lexi said confidently. "He says he'll be stronger than he was before the accident."

Lexi and Peggy's conversation was interrupted by the youth pastor. "Hello, girls. How are you tonight?"

"Hi, Pastor Lake! What're we doing tonight?" Lexi asked.

"It's a surprise."

"I've never seen him so secretive," Jennifer commented when Pastor Lake had left them.

Pastor Lake's easy smile and casual manner were exactly what appealed to the teenagers. He was never critical of them or judgmental, always willing to listen to their problems.

He stood at the front of the room now and smiled broadly. "First of all, I must remind you that soon we'll have to elect officers for this organization. Think about who you'd like to nominate. We'll also need to elect people for snack and program committees. Tonight, however, I have something else to discuss. I realize you were probably expecting some special activity tonight. Well, there isn't one."

There were groans and moans throughout the room.

"I wanted you all to come tonight so I could let you in on a new program I'm developing for our church."

"Is this going to be boring, or what?" Tressa Williams whispered.

Anna Marie scowled at Tressa for her rudeness, but Tressa ignored her.

Pastor Lake had heard Tressa's comment. "I hope not. As most of you know, I worked with the youth at my last church. But I also had another responsibility. I was an alcohol addiction counselor. Now I've been asked to begin a rehabilitation program here. The prospect is very exciting for me."

"Aren't there already programs like that in Cedar River?" someone asked.

"There are many excellent programs in this community, but most of them are strictly for adults. Since my ministry is with the youth of the church, I'm targeting the program for teenagers and young adults who may not have as many choices or places to go to get help with their addictions."

"Teenagers?"

"That's right. Most people don't realize how many teenagers and young adults are secretly drinking."

"Oh, great. A crusade." Peggy squirmed in her chair. "He got us all here tonight to tell us this? What a waste of time!"

"Shhhh," Lexi whispered. "Give him a chance."

"Yeah, right," Peggy answered. "Who wants to hear about his ideas on teenagers and alcohol?" She slumped into the chair and covered her face with her hands.

Lexi thought the whole concept sounded fascinating. The more Pastor Lake talked, the more interested she became.

"Studies vary," he continued, "but at least one survey indicates that the average age for a young person to start drinking is twelve."

"Twelve years old!" Binky blurted. "They're children!"

Pastor Lake heard her and smiled. "We tend to think that, Binky. But if you talked to a twelve-year-old, you'd realize *they* don't think they're children. Twelve-year-olds are often trying to prove to others that they're older and more mature than their age would indicate. Some kids start to drink to prove that they're grown up."

"All that proves is that they're even younger and dumber than they thought," Binky muttered.

"Alcohol is an easily accessible drug for young people. Children can find it in their own homes or get it from their peers. It is the drug of choice for young people."

"But alcohol isn't a drug," someone piped from the last row.

"Oh, but it is," Pastor Lake corrected. "Alcohol is as much a mood-altering drug as marijuana or cocaine."

"It doesn't *seem* as bad," Egg said.

"That's only because it's been *approved* by our society. Once people are of age, they're able to buy alcohol and use it. That doesn't change the fact that it is a drug." Pastor Lake's expression grew even more serious. "Studies show that many teenagers who commit suicide have been drinking at the time."

Lexi heard Peggy's sharp intake of breath.

"But teenagers can't become alcoholics," Tressa Williams spoke up. "That's something that happens to adults. Right?"

"I wish it were true, Tressa. The fact is, a teen's body isn't mature yet. For this reason they can become addicted more quickly than adults."

"I'm not sure I buy all this," Minda said. "Is it

really such a big deal? I've seen alcohol served at high-school parties, but I've never seen anyone all that drunk."

"Maybe not, but it's a start. Many teens have their first drink in their own home. Often parents who keep alcohol in the house don't keep it out of reach of their children. We've spent many years trying to prevent the use of illegal drugs. I feel now it's time to spend some time and energy on the problem of alcohol abuse."

"I can't believe we have to listen to this," Peggy grumbled. "I should have stayed home." Pastor Lake glanced in her direction, obviously disturbed, but said nothing to Peggy.

"Be quiet." Egg poked her with the toe of his tennis shoe. "Some of us are trying to listen."

"The administration and faculty of Cedar River High School are in full agreement with me," Pastor Lake went on. "Once we get the program up and running in our church, I'll go to the high school to give lectures to educate the students about alcohol abuse."

Peggy shook her head in disbelief.

"I'd like to present something to the grade school as well, warning younger children about the traps they can fall into.

"We're losing some of the best and most valuable resources we have in this country—our young people. Every year a large number of teenagers die in alcohol-related car accidents. That's a waste we simply cannot afford. If there's anything we can do to put the brakes on this sort of tragedy, I believe it's our responsibility to do it." He looked around the room for some response. "Have any of you ever ridden in a car with a driver who'd been drinking?"

There was absolute silence in the room. Then, slowly, hands began to go up. Lexi was shocked to see how many in their group had at one time or another been in a car with a driver who'd been drinking.

"Sometimes you just can't help it," someone in the back row piped. "I mean, how can you get home if the person you came with has been drinking?"

"Good question. But it's never a good idea to get into a car with a driver who has had too much to drink. Sometimes that's hard to determine. How about calling your parents?"

"My folks would kill me if they knew I'd gone to a party where there was booze!" someone spoke up.

"You could call a friend, someone who wasn't at the party. Or call a trusted adult you'd feel comfortable telling about the situation." Pastor Lake was intense. "If any of you ever get into such a predicament, *don't get into the car*. Call your parents or a friend. Call me. I'd be glad to pick you up and take you home. *Never, ever get into a car with a drunk driver*."

"What are you going to do to begin this program?" Brian James asked.

"There are hospitals and centers that offer inpatient and outpatient treatment," Pastor Lake explained. "We don't have the facilities or the staff for that. What I'd like to see at this church is a support group.

"It would be a group that meets regularly, and its goal would be to help alcoholics, or anyone with a drinking problem, to remain sober. The group would offer support and friendship. Their job would be to let the recovering alcoholic or the drinking teenager know that he or she is not alone; that there are others out there struggling as well.

"A problem is easier to bear if it is shared. We all need an understanding friend to talk to. That's what support groups offer. We aren't a hospital. We aren't a treatment center. But what better place to find friendship, fellowship, support, love and prayer than at a church? We already know how to provide these things. Now we'll target an audience—teenage alcohol abusers."

Peggy slumped lower and lower in her seat.

Lexi had begun to mull over the vision of Peggy sneaking into the costume room with a flask of alcohol. Before, she had hated to admit that her friend may have a problem. Now, she was sure she had one, and hoped that Pastor Lake would be able to help her.

"What about the teen's parents?" asked a timid voice from the back row. "Would they have to know about this . . . problem?"

"It's important for a person to be able to talk to his or her parents about the issue. It's a battle no one should have to fight alone. A supportive family can be a great deal of help."

Peggy was beginning to glance at her watch every few minutes.

"What's the matter?" Lexi asked.

"I promised my mom I'd be home at eight-thirty. It's twenty after. I'd better get going. See you tomorrow." Without another word, Peggy slipped from her seat and left.

"Where is she going?" Egg leaned toward Lexi.

"She said she had to be home by eight-thirty."

"Mm-m-m. She didn't mention that before."

Lexi remained silent. There was nothing to say. She didn't want to expose her friend's problem, although she was sure others suspected it as well.

The conversation was serious but animated as Lexi and her friends left the church.

"That was heavy stuff," Binky admitted. "I always thought alcohol problems were for really wild kids who hung out on street corners and stole hubcaps or something. I didn't realize regular young people like us could have that kind of problem."

"Regular young people can have all sorts of problems," Jennifer pointed out. "I'm dyslexic. Lexi has a handicapped brother . . ."

"But, alcohol?" Binky made a face. "It stinks. It couldn't taste good. Who'd want to bother with it?"

"Teens who want to get away from problems," Egg said wisely. "It's easier to run away or hide from a problem than to face it head-on. That's what alcohol does for people. It helps them escape into another world."

The group walked in the direction of the city park as they talked.

"I'm sure you're right," Jennifer said thoughtfully. "I know some who have tried drinking, though, that don't seem to have any really big problems."

"Remember what Pastor Lake said about peer pressure? Sometimes people drink to be popular, to be part of the gang. Once they try to stop, they can't.

They've already become addicted."

"People will do just about anything to be popular, won't they?" Binky's tone was one of disgust.

"I've done some pretty stupid things just to be popular," Egg reminded his sister. "When I was wanting Minda to notice me, I thought about taking steroids just so I could bulk up." He shuddered. "When I think about it now, I'm sure I must have been crazy. But at the time, it almost made sense."

"That was a close call, Egg," Lexi said. "I guess it shows how foolish we can act when we want something badly enough."

They all walked silently through the park, each lost in their own thoughts.

The winding paths were quiet, except for night sounds in the air—the rustling trees, crickets in the grass, the distant hum of motors on the highway. It was dark except for the soft golden glow of an occasional street lamp.

Binky shivered and clutched her arms to her chest. "Let's not walk too deep into the park tonight. I've heard there are a lot of creepy people hanging out here since school started."

It was a rumor Lexi hadn't heard. "What do you mean, Binky?"

"Older guys. High school dropouts. The guys who do drugs and drink. After what Pastor Lake told us tonight, I really don't want to meet up with any of them."

"Do we know any of these people?" Lexi wondered aloud.

"Not personally. But you know several dropped out of school this year. They work at car washes, gas stations, any place that will hire someone without a high school education."

"I've heard they *do* spend a lot of time drinking," Egg added. "I've seen them too. A couple of guys who were in Harry Cramer's class hang out in the park at night."

This was all news to Lexi. Her world suddenly seemed small and sheltered.

The park was different at night too. Almost eerie. It was full of shadows, and every branch and twig seemed to creak. They walked past the statue of the founder of Cedar River. Even in her somber mood, Lexi smiled, remembering the day the statue was beheaded and they'd found the culprit.

"Eeek!" a squeak escaped Binky. "What was that?"

"Don't worry," Egg comforted, "it was just a bat."

"A bat! Let's get out of here!" Binky squealed. "This place gives me the creeps."

Lexi was inclined to agree.

As they neared the edge of the park, they saw a group of young men gathered beneath a street light. They were all strangers to Lexi. They wore torn jeans and tattered T-shirts in contrast to expensive high-tops. All seemed to be smoking cigarettes.

"There they are," Egg said matter-of-factly.

Then Lexi noticed two or three girls in the group. Suddenly a familiar face emerged from the shadows.

"Peggy!" Egg gasped under his breath.

Jennifer, Lexi, Egg, and Binky froze in their tracks. They stared at the group gathered around the light, talking and laughing. One of the boys took a final drag on his cigarette, threw it to the ground and crushed it out with his heel.

Peggy began talking animatedly with a young man at the edge of the group. She gestured with her hands, deeply engrossed in conversation. She dug deep into the pocket of her jeans and handed something to the young man. In exchange, he gave her a paper sack.

"What is she doing with bad news like that?" Jennifer asked, furious. "Is she crazy?"

"I thought she had to be *home* at eight-thirty," Binky said.

"When did Peggy start taking tours through the park at night? I don't like the look of this," Egg said.

Lexi noticed that Egg's voice was quavering. Suddenly, she was frightened. She wished Todd were there to take her hand, to tell her that everything would be all right.

"Let's get out of here," she blurted.

Lexi felt Egg's hand on her back, pushing her toward the way they'd come. They were all out of breath by the time they reached Lexi's house. She could see by the glow of the street light that Binky's hands were shaking now, too.

"What could Peggy want from that bunch?" Binky asked.

"I think she's gone crazy," Jennifer spoke to no one in particular. "That's the only explanation. Chad's death must have sent her off the deep end. Why else would she be hanging out with those guys? Why else would she be lying to us?"

Not one of them could answer her questions.

Chapter Eight

Lexi awoke early the next morning. She lay on her back, her hands tucked behind her head, and stared at the ceiling.

Had it been a dream? Or had she really seen Peggy in the park with those strangers? It made no sense at all. What was she doing there? Why had she lied to them?

Peggy obviously didn't need to be home at eight-thirty. She must have planned to meet those people in the park. The whole idea gave Lexi the chills.

I'll have to talk to Mom about it, Lexi thought. Mrs. Leighton always had a stable perspective on things. Even though she was of another generation, it seemed to Lexi that she understood teenagers better than anyone else.

A knock on the door startled Lexi. Her mother poked her head through the doorway. "Are you awake?"

"Yeah, Mom." Lexi stretched and sat upright. "I didn't need an alarm clock this morning."

"That's a switch. Got something on your mind?"

"How did you know?"

"That's the way it is for me." Mrs. Leighton sat

down on the edge of Lexi's bed. "When I go to sleep at night with something plaguing my mind, I usually awake with those same thoughts the next morning."

"Oh. I *have* been thinking about something."

"Want to talk about it?"

Lexi wasn't sure she wanted to tell her mother about the scene she'd witnessed last night until she knew why Peggy had been there.

"I've been worrying about Peggy, that's all," Lexi said finally. "She's been acting strangely again."

"Oh? I guess it's not so surprising," Mrs. Leighton said. "Peggy's been through a lot in the past few months. More trauma than most girls her age have had to bear."

"She was really odd at youth group last night. Pastor Lake is starting a support group for teenage alcoholics at our church. He wanted to explain the program to our group, since we will be involved in helping with it. I thought it was really interesting, but Peggy was bored and kept making rude comments."

Mrs. Leighton listened intently, not saying anything.

"Finally, Peggy said she had to go home. Said she'd promised to be home at eight-thirty."

"Is that so strange?"

"No, but I don't think Peggy really had to be home at eight-thirty." The scene in the park flashed into Lexi's mind. "In fact, I'm *sure* she didn't have to be home. She just wanted to leave the group."

"I see."

"Peggy isn't the same girl she used to be, Mom. She's acting weird. She's unpredictable."

Before her mother could comment, the telephone rang. Lexi grabbed it before the second ring. "Leighton residence. Lexi speaking."

"Good morning!" Todd's voice was unmistakable.

"Todd! Why are you calling so early?" Lexi tried to hide the smile in her voice. "I'm just getting up!"

"You don't understand hospital schedules, Lexi. I've already had breakfast. In a couple of hours, they'll be serving me lunch."

Lexi yawned into the phone. "I'm glad I'm on my schedule and not yours, Todd."

"Okay, but I'll be on a schedule like yours soon."

"What did you say?"

"I said I'll be on a schedule like yours soon."

"You mean you're leaving the hospital?"

His laughter bubbled across the line. "Today, Lexi. I'm coming home today!"

Lexi squealed with delight. "It's Todd, Mom. He's coming home. Today!"

Mrs. Leighton smiled. "Great. Tell Todd I'm delighted."

"The doctor says I'm really doing well, Lexi. He says my progress has been amazing."

"When are you getting out?" Lexi asked breathlessly.

"After lunch. I have to go to physical therapy this morning; I'm waiting for them to come for me now. I'll be able to do some of my therapy at home, and go to rehab for the rest. The doctor thinks I'll make more progress with my family and friends around me."

"You'll be home by the time school is out, then?" Lexi could hardly imagine it.

"I'll be there. Are you coming to see me?"

"Of course!" Lexi's eyes were shining. "Oh, Todd, I've missed you so much. I'm so glad you're coming home."

"No happier than I am. I'd better let you go, Lexi. I'll be waiting for you tonight. Bye."

Lexi gently hung up the phone. "He's coming home, Mom! Isn't that wonderful news?" She jumped out of bed and danced around the room, grabbing her mother for a spin.

"He'll be there after school, tonight. Can you believe it?"

Mrs. Leighton smiled at her daughter. "Sounds like I'd better do some baking. Todd will want some chocolate chip cookies, don't you think?"

"Dozens of them," Lexi agreed. She stopped in front of the closet. "I'd better get dressed or I'll be late for school. I can't wait to tell everyone Todd's coming home!"

————

Benjamin was sitting at the kitchen table eating french toast when Lexi bounded down the stairs two at a time.

"Todd's coming home, Ben. Isn't that wonderful?" She gave her little brother a noisy smack on his forehead.

Ben made a face and wiped away the dampness. "Girls are weird," he stated flatly. "They like to kiss."

"Has a girl at school tried to kiss you, Ben?"

"Yes." Ben frowned. "All the girls want to kiss Ben."

"That's because you're so handsome and charming, Ben."

He sighed wearily. "Yes. Handsome and charming."

Lexi grinned at her mother. "What do you think, Mom?"

"It's the price Ben has to pay for being such a sweetheart."

Ben made a face and covered his eyes with his hands. Lexi kissed the tempting little cowlick on the top of his head.

"All the men in my life are handsome and charming. I can hardly wait to see the one who's coming home tonight!"

———

Lexi caught up to Jennifer and Binky as they walked to school. "Where are Egg and Peggy?" she asked.

"Egg had to go in early this morning. Peggy'd already left when we came by," Binky explained.

"Since you weren't on the porch, we thought you'd already gone, too."

"I got a telephone call this morning that made me late." Lexi could feel her heart skipping a beat. "Guess who it was."

"We don't have any idea."

"Todd! He's coming home. Tonight!"

Binky emitted a piercing squeal.

Jennifer flung her arms around Lexi and whirled her around in the middle of the sidewalk.

"I am so happy," Binky said. "I thought Todd was a goner for sure when he had that accident. And now he's coming home. It's wonderful!"

"He still has a long way to go," Lexi reminded her. "But according to the doctors, he's doing exceptionally well. Let's hurry. There're lots of people who will want to hear the good news."

Lexi told everyone she met all day long. "Todd's coming home. He's getting out of the hospital today!"

When Egg heard the news, he gave Lexi a big kiss on the forehead. Matt Windsor put his arm around her and squeezed her tight. Even Minda gave her a thumbs-up sign.

Mrs. Waverly wiped a tear from the corner of her eye and said, "I'm so happy."

By the end of the day, Lexi was sure every student and teacher had stopped to speak to her, and sent their good wishes to Todd.

"Aren't you taking any books home?" Binky asked as she watched Lexi stuff hers into her locker. "I've got a lot of homework tonight."

"I'm taking the night off to celebrate."

"You're going to be at Todd's all evening?"

"Probably not. He'll be tired. I'm just too giddy and excited to study. Besides, I have a study hall first period tomorrow. I can do what I need to then."

"Be sure to tell him hi for us," Binky instructed. "And tell him we love him."

The front door was open and the Winston family car was in the driveway when Lexi arrived. Mike Winston's motorcycle was parked near the garage.

Lexi tapped on the door. She could hear laughter inside.

Todd's father came to the door. His eyes were brighter than Lexi had seen them in a long time. "There you are. We've been waiting for you." He escorted Lexi into the living room. Todd was sitting in his father's easy chair near the fireplace.

She went to his side and took his hand. "Welcome home, Todd."

"He looks wonderful, doesn't he, Lexi?" Mrs. Winston enthused.

"Sure does. He looks just great."

"You're going to have a swollen head, Todd," Mike Winston sauntered into the living room with a sandwich. "If everybody keeps telling you how good you look, you're going to be awfully hard to live with."

"How does it feel to be home?" Lexi dropped onto the footstool near Todd's chair.

"It's the most beautiful place in the world." Todd grinned impishly at his mother. "In fact, I like it here so much I might even be willing to dust and vacuum just to prove my point."

Mrs. Winston put her hands to her face. "Can I believe my ears? Todd, offering to dust . . . and vacuum?"

"He must be deliriously happy to be home," Mike teased. "Or else that accident did something more to his head than we realized."

Despite the laughter and good-natured joking, Lexi noticed that Todd was suddenly quiet.

"Are you tired, Todd?"

"I hate to admit it, but I am. They worked me for hours in physical therapy today."

Mrs. Winston stood up briskly. "I'm sorry, Todd. Maybe you should be resting."

"Ohhh, Mom," he protested. Then he put his head back. "Well, maybe, for a little while."

Lexi glanced at her watch. "I'd better be going, Todd. It's really good to have you home." She stood to leave.

"I'm sorry, Lexi."

"There's nothing to be sorry about. I'll see you tomorrow."

"I'm not going anywhere," Mike said bluntly. "We've got a lot of things to catch up on, little brother."

Lexi smiled at the two. "See you. Thanks, Mrs. Winston," she said to Todd's mother.

"Goodbye, dear."

Lexi slipped out the door and stood on the sidewalk. There was a soft breeze, and she lifted her face to the sky. "Thank you, God, for bringing him home."

"If she blows that line one more time, I'm going to scream." Minda was looking cross-eyed at Peggy as they rehearsed their lines for *Macbeth*.

It hadn't been a good rehearsal. Everybody was getting more and more tense and irritated with Peggy's inability to get through a scene without messing it up.

Lexi had her mouth full of straight pins. She was making a valiant attempt to take the necessary tucks and darts to fit the costumes to the assorted shapes and sizes. Whenever someone was not rehearsing their lines, Lexi pulled them aside to mark their costumes. Behind the scenes, she was busy sewing—lengthening or shortening dresses and tunics, crafting caps and hats from scraps of velvet or felt and generally having a difficult time making twentieth-century teenagers look like eleventh-century noblemen.

"Ouch!" Binky squawked as Lexi poked a pin through the fabric and into her flesh. "Watch it!"

"Sorry," Lexi muttered. "Quit squirming."

"I can't help it. We're all tired of waiting for Peggy to say her lines."

Lexi glanced over at Peggy and Mrs. Waverly. "What seems to be the problem?"

"Peggy can't remember her lines. She keeps messing up. I suppose I shouldn't blame her. This Shakespeare stuff is hard. But the rest of us are doing okay. She's the only one who's mixed up. Sometimes I wonder if she knows what's going on at all."

Lexi made no comment. Peggy Madison was a smart girl. Granted, *Macbeth* might be the hardest play they'd ever done, but if anyone could understand it, surely it was Peggy!

Lexi picked up her tape measure and pins and moved toward Peggy. Lady Macbeth had more costume changes than most of the other characters. If Lexi was going to get all the costumes completed, she'd have to get going on Peggy's soon.

"Try it again, Peggy," Mrs. Waverly was saying patiently. "Go slowly this time. Think about what you're saying."

"But my tongue gets tangled up in these awful words," Peggy complained. "No one talks like this."

"No, Peggy, but this is acting. You can do it. Try again."

Peggy sighed and picked up her play book. "Oh, never shall sun that morrow see! Your face, my Thane, is as a book where men may read strange matters. To beguile the time, look like the time; bear welcome in your eye, your hand, your tongue; look like the innocent flower, but be the serpent under't." Peggy stopped, her face flushed pink. "How was that?"

"Much better, my dear," Mrs. Waverly said. She gave Peggy a pat on the arm. "You didn't tangle up any of the words this time."

"But I didn't understand what I was saying," Peggy wailed. "What does that mean, 'To beguile the time, look like the time?' "

"It means to deceive. Look as people expect you to under the circumstances. Lady Macbeth is telling her husband to look like an innocent flower, but in reality be the snake that's lurking under the blossoms."

"Then why didn't Shakespeare just say that?" Peggy asked.

"He did," Mrs. Waverly said with a laugh. "In his own words, according to the language of his day."

"Come on, Peggy," the boy who was playing the messenger yelled from across the stage. "We're only on the fifth scene, Act One. Let's keep moving. Aren't you ever going to get the hang of this?"

Peggy's jaw set stubbornly. "I'm doing the best I can. I have a . . . headache."

"Oh, poor baby," someone called from behind stage.

"We're never going to get through this play today," another moaned.

Lexi could sense the tension building. She saw it in Peggy's expression. She'd stumbled clumsily on the cables that crisscrossed at the back of the stage. Before rehearsal started, Peggy had refused to go over her lines. Now she was paying the price.

Matt Windsor and the witches were glaring at Peggy irately. Tim Anders and Brian James played tic-tac-toe on a piece of unpainted backdrop. The boys cast as Donalbain and Lennox were sitting on the floor with their backs to the wall, reading auto mechanics and weight-lifting magazines. Peggy's attitude had managed to affect the entire cast.

Mrs. Waverly wore a worried expression. "Perhaps you should all go home for now," she suggested. "I'm sure everything will go better tomorrow. Matt, you have a lot of lines to learn, maybe you'd like to stay and work with me for a while. The rest of you are excused."

With the first energy she'd shown all day, Peggy darted off the stage and down the stairs.

By the expression on Mrs. Waverly's face, Lexi could tell she wasn't at all sure that things *would* be better tomorrow.

Chapter Nine

Lexi stretched her legs beneath the dining room table at Todd's house. It was wonderful to be studying together again as they had always done in the past. Lexi'd once feared those days were over. Now she met Todd's gaze.

He winked at her. "What are you thinking about, Lexi? You've got an odd expression on your face."

"I was thinking about how happy I am," she admitted. "I like sitting across the table from you, studying together. I thought right after your accident that we might never be able to do this again."

"Oh." Todd's face clouded. "I'd wondered too, I guess. But that doesn't mean I *enjoy* studying right now." He stretched and yawned. "Maybe I'm not ready to go back to school yet."

"When do you think the doctor will give you the go ahead? Next week?"

"I doubt it. Even though he's encouraged me to keep up with my schoolwork, he hasn't given me any deadline for getting back into classes. That's all right with me. I hate to admit it, but I'm beginning to get nervous about returning to school."

"Why? Everyone is anxious for you to come back."

"Sure, but it's still going to be tough." His gaze dropped. "I'm not an athlete anymore, Lexi. I'm awkward and clumsy. There's a lot to learn over again . . ."

"You're worried about being clumsy?" Lexi looked incredulous. "Todd, everyone will be so happy to have you back, you could knock over every desk and no one would complain. We were all afraid you'd never walk again, remember?"

"I know. You're right. My brother Mike tells me I'm ungrateful. He says I'm lucky I didn't break my neck."

"Your brother doesn't talk much, but he certainly says what's on his mind."

"Do you know who he reminds me of?" Todd asked, grinning. "Jennifer Golden. Mike and Jennifer are a lot alike. You always know what they think and where they stand on an issue."

"When I first met Jennifer, her bluntness startled me," Lexi admitted. "Now I appreciate it. She's honest, up front. You don't have to wonder if Jennifer likes something or not. She's perfectly happy to tell you." Lexi propped her chin in her hands and stared out the window. "I've really learned a lot from my friends in Cedar River, even though some of them haven't been nearly as easy to get to know as Jennifer."

"Like who?"

"Peggy Madison, for one."

"How is she as Lady Macbeth?"

Lexi took a long moment to answer. "Frankly, I'm worried about her."

"She's doing that badly?"

Lexi nodded her head. "Yes."

"Peggy's a smart girl. She'll catch on."

Lexi couldn't hold it in any longer. She told Todd about running in to Peggy in the park. "Those were *weird* guys she was with, Todd. None of us could figure out why she'd be with them, especially after telling us that she had to go home."

"That *is* strange," Todd agreed. "Did you know any of them?"

"Egg thought one or two had been in Harry Cramer's class before dropping out."

"Maybe one of them was a friend of Peggy's," Todd suggested. "It's a big school. Peggy could have had a class with him."

Lexi thought back. "It's possible, but I doubt it."

"The only way you're going to find out is to ask Peggy," Todd suggested.

"Oh, Todd, Peggy's difficult to talk to these days. Besides, she didn't know we were there. She'd think we were spying on her if I asked."

"How's the homework progressing?" Todd's mother had just come home from work. She was wearing a navy suit and a soft pink blouse. Her hair and nails were perfectly groomed. Lexi had always admired Todd's mother. Even though she worked outside their home, she always had time for her sons and their friends.

"Slowly," Todd said, pushing his books away. "Maybe my brain is turning to mush."

Mrs. Winston laughed and patted Todd on the shoulder. "Good try. I think your brain is just fine. You've just gotten lazy."

"Lazy? You call all the work I've been doing in

physical therapy being lazy?"

"No, but you haven't been doing that much schoolwork. I think it's time you went back to school."

"Did you talk to the doctor today? Did he give you a date?"

"Not yet. We'll ask him at your next appointment. I know you must be getting restless." She turned to Lexi. "Thanks for coming over to study with Todd, Lexi. He's been driving me crazy.

"How's your little brother?" Mrs. Winston asked, changing the subject. "Is Ben happy at the Academy this year?"

"He's so eager to get to school, Mother has trouble getting him to eat breakfast. He thinks there's no place in the world like the Academy."

Mrs. Winston was about to comment when the doorbell rang. For a moment it sounded as if the mechanism were jammed. It chimed over and over again. Then, before anyone could reach the door, Egg and Binky burst in, wide-eyed and excited.

Egg came skidding into the dining room at such a pace he nearly bumped into Mrs. Winston.

"Is there some kind of an emergency?" Mrs. Winston asked, concern in her voice.

Todd and Lexi grinned at each other. To the McNaughtons, most things in life were an emergency.

Egg paced back and forth across the living room, his long slender fingers moving agitatedly. Binky perched on the edge of the sofa, her hands clenched together tightly. Her face was pale beneath the thin scattering of freckles across the bridge of her nose.

Even though Todd and Lexi were accustomed to Egg and Binky's emergencies, neither of them had ever seen the two quite this worked up.

"You'd better tell us what's going on," Todd urged. "And start at the beginning."

"Well, Binky and I were on our way home, and we saw Pastor Lake's car at the church, so we decided to stop in and say hello."

"He was in his office doing some research for the support group he's starting."

"The one for teen alcoholics?" Todd asked.

"That's it. He had stacks of material all over his desk. He was trying to put together a handout for the youth group—to help us understand a little more about the teenage alcoholic."

"Binky and I must have looked interested, because he offered to show us the material. It was still in rough draft, but he wanted our response."

"I started to read the information," Binky said, "and I couldn't stop. It described the symptoms and behavior of teenage drinkers." She became more pale as she spoke, and her gray-green eyes grew wide and expressive. "I got cold inside and I had this scary feeling in the pit of my stomach. I looked at Egg and realized he was thinking the same thing I was."

"We're not mind-readers, Binky," Todd prodded. "What was so upsetting?"

"There were stories, case studies, in which kids talked about drinking. One girl said that the first time she got drunk she felt better than she ever had before. She felt strong and brave. She forgot about all the problems she had in her life at home. She wanted to forget those problems for longer and longer periods of time, so she kept on drinking."

"Get to the point, Binky," Lexi urged.

"Everything that Egg and I read made us realize that *Peggy's* been behaving just like the teens described in Pastor Lake's material."

"Peggy?" Todd's voice was sharp.

"Yes," Egg affirmed. "The symptoms include things like rebelliousness and hanging out with a bad, older crowd. If anyone has things in her life they'd like to forget, it's Peggy."

"To say that Peggy is an alcoholic is a pretty strong conclusion," Mrs. Winston interjected.

"I know. That's what scares us," Binky said. "Pastor Lake showed us an article with a list of things to watch for in teen alcoholics. It was as if the list were describing Peggy. It said one sign is when a teenager begins hanging out with a new, tougher crowd. One who drinks will seek out others who drink. And a younger teenager will seek out an older one as a source of alcohol."

"Seeing Peggy with some older boys in the park doesn't mean she's an alcoholic," Lexi protested.

"Her behavior has changed," Binky pointed out. "You have to admit that. She's started to argue with her mom, something she never used to do, at least not around us."

Lexi couldn't deny the fact.

"The article also said that teenage drinkers sometimes suffer from depression, and . . ." Binky paused for emphasis, "sometimes they have unexplained injuries."

"You mean when she tripped on the hem of her robe and bruised her leg?" Todd asked. "Lexi told me about it."

"Yeah. But her story didn't add up. For one thing, she doesn't have a long robe," Binky said.

"I think you're making too much of this," Todd said. "It isn't a mystery to be solved, after all, like when someone's been kidnapped. This is our friend Peggy you're talking about."

"She's not the same person she used to be, Todd," Egg said. "You haven't been around her lately to see the changes, the little things. It's hard to put your finger on all of them, but the changes are there."

Lexi wanted to argue, to say that their imaginations were working overtime, but she couldn't. What Egg and Binky were saying made sense. Peggy *had* changed. And alcohol could certainly be the cause. After all, Lexi had seen Peggy drinking something in the costume room, and they had all seen her irrational behavior when they stayed overnight recently at her house.

"I realize that teenagers cringe at too much adult input," Mrs. Winston said, her expression somber, "but, this is a very serious problem. If there's any chance at all that Peggy might be having trouble with alcohol, someone should talk to her parents. They need to know about this. If her behavior has altered this radically, she needs help."

"Talk to her family?" Binky swallowed, and looked at her brother. "We were so frightened and excited, we just had to come here and tell someone." Her voice was timid. "Maybe we shouldn't have spilled our thoughts. Maybe we've jumped to conclusions."

"No. You did the right thing," Mrs. Winston affirmed. "Don't think for a moment that you didn't. If no one wants to talk to Peggy's mother and father, I will."

The four teenagers looked at one another. Peggy might never forgive them for interfering like this.

"Mrs. Winston," Lexi said softly, "I'd like to have the opportunity to talk to Peggy before you go to her family. Maybe we're mistaken."

Egg opened his mouth to protest, then thought better of it.

"I would like to tell Peggy what we think and what we're going to do. I owe her that much," Lexi repeated.

"Well . . . I suppose that would be all right." Mrs. Winston sounded reluctant. "But you will have to do it right away."

"Oh yes. I would go crazy worrying about it, if I didn't. We could also go to Pastor Lake. He's had experience with this, and maybe he could tell us what to do next."

Mrs. Winston considered Lexi's suggestion. "Maybe you're right. A professional is probably the person to consult. He'll know just what to do. But something should be done immediately. If Peggy is in any sort of danger—physical, emotional or mental—we can't let it go on any longer."

Lexi felt a huge lump in her throat. She'd never been so nervous in her entire life.

"I'll go speak to Peggy right now." Lexi got up from the table. She took Todd's hand, and he squeezed hers firmly.

"Let me know what happens," he said softly. "I'll be waiting . . . and praying."

Lexi went out the door and down the stairs with

a heavy heart. Egg and Binky followed her.

"Lexi, wait up," Egg said. "We want to come, too."

"It might be better if I talked to Peggy alone. She might be more willing to talk to just one of us." Lexi's steps faltered. "Maybe I'm doing the wrong thing by talking to her at all."

"We're the ones who've read the material, Lexi," Binky pointed out. "We've known Peggy a long time. I think we should be there, too."

The only light they could see in the Madison house was in the living room. Lexi tapped nervously on the door. Egg and Binky stood behind her, shuffling their feet.

Oh, God, help me do this right, Lexi prayed silently. *Give me the words I need to say.*

Peggy opened the door and peered outside. "What are you guys doing here?" she asked. "Come on in."

"Are your folks home?" Binky asked.

"Not right now. They'll be back later. Why?"

"We wanted to talk to you."

"About the lousy job I've been doing on the play, no doubt." She gestured to the play book on the sofa. "I've been learning my lines, but it's hard for me to concentrate lately. I don't even know why I tried out. It was stupid of me. When I go to rehearsals I wish I were home."

"You'll do fine, Peggy, I know you will," Lexi encouraged.

"I'm glad you think so, Lexi."

"Peggy, we need to talk to you," Egg blurted, his voice quavering.

"Why so serious?" Peggy asked. "You guys look like you have bad news."

Lexi sat down on the sofa. "Sit down, Peggy."

"What is going on?" Peggy demanded.

"We've been worried about you lately, Peggy," Lexi began. "We wanted to talk to you about it."

Peggy rolled her eyes. "Somebody's always worried about me. People still bring up Chad, just when I think I've finally put his death behind me."

"It's not about that," Lexi assured her.

"Well, what is it then?"

"We think you've been acting strangely," Binky blurted. "We're afraid something's wrong."

"Wrong? What could be wrong?"

Lexi saw a flicker of alarm in Peggy's eyes.

"We saw you in the park the other night, Peggy— after youth group," Lexi began slowly. "After you'd said you had to be home at eight-thirty."

Peggy's eyes darted from side to side. She shifted uncomfortably on the sofa. "So what?"

"What were you doing?" Egg asked.

Peggy looked threatened. "Just what do *you* think I was doing?"

"We think you were buying liquor, Peggy," Egg said bluntly.

Lexi wished that Egg and Binky had not come with her. This was turning out all wrong. They were putting Peggy on the defensive.

"You came all the way over here to tell me that? Great. Some friends you are. Thanks a lot." Peggy was indignant. "I went for a walk in the park. I met somebody who was in school last spring. I stopped to talk. The next thing I know, three of my best friends are accusing me of buying alcohol. That makes me feel like you really trust me."

"We didn't mean to insult you, Peggy," Egg said. "It's just that we read this stuff that Pastor Lake had on his desk . . ."

Lexi wished she could tell Egg to be quiet, but it was too late.

"So you read about something and decided I had the problem. Oh, great. When did you become a therapist, Egg?" Peggy turned to Lexi. "And you came with them. Do you believe them, instead of me? Lexi Leighton, how could you? I thought you were a friend of mine." Peggy stood up. She was trembling. "Get out of my house—all of you."

"Peggy, we didn't mean any harm . . ."

"Get out. You're no friends of mine." Peggy pointed to the door. "Get out!" Her face contorted with rage.

Lexi was shaken and Binky was sobbing as they walked out the door. Egg followed them, his head high, his jaw determined. He turned back to face Peggy. "We *are* your friends, Peggy. We care about you."

"If you were my friends, you would never have come here to humiliate me!" she screamed.

The door slammed in Egg's face.

"We shouldn't have come. We shouldn't have come," Binky kept repeating.

Lexi hung on to Binky, trying to console her.

Whatever made them think they could handle something like this alone? Had they alienated Peggy forever?

It was Egg who was in control. "Something is definitely wrong with Peggy. If it's not alcohol, it's something else. We may have made a mistake trying to handle this on our own, but I know Peggy is lying."

"How do you know, Egg?" Binky was still sobbing.

"Peggy had been drinking tonight, Binky. I could smell alcohol on her breath. I guess Mrs. Winston was right. We should have had an adult help us. Tomorrow we'll go and talk to Pastor Lake."

Chapter Ten

Saturday morning Lexi awoke early. She'd slept very little. Her eyes felt scratchy and her muscles ached. She was almost sick at the thought of what had transpired last night.

Why had she thought they were wise enough to handle a situation like that without help? She'd blundered into the confrontation with Peggy without even talking to God about it. "You think you're smart, Lexi Leighton," she muttered to herself in the mirror. "Well, you've blown it now."

The doorbell rang. Before she got downstairs, Lexi knew who it would be. When she opened the door, Egg and Binky walked in slowly.

"Are you ready to go to the church?" Egg asked.

He'd really taken charge of the situation. Lexi was glad. She felt as if all her energy had been drained away.

"I don't know if I can face Pastor Lake," Binky said with a moan. "I've been thinking about it all night. Maybe we've made a terrible mistake."

Lexi thought through all they had witnessed recently—Peggy's fall, the scene in the costume room, her failure to memorize lines for her part in the play, the arguing with her mother, the outbursts at her friends. Perhaps they wanted to overlook these things, didn't want to admit something was wrong, but as much as she hated it, Lexi believed they were right about their conclusion. There was no mistake.

The telephone rang and Lexi heard her mother answer it in the kitchen.

Mrs. Leighton walked into the living room. "Lexi, that was Peggy's mother on the phone."

They all held their breath.

"Is something wrong?" Lexi asked.

"Peggy's been taken to the hospital."

"What?" Egg bounded to his feet.

"The doctors believe Peggy is suffering from an overdose of alcohol."

Lexi's jaw dropped.

Mrs. Leighton looked intently at the three. "Did any of you suspect that Peggy had a drinking problem?"

Binky burst into tears. "We should have figured it out sooner. Now she'll probably die."

Mrs. Leighton put her hand on Binky's trembling shoulder. "Peggy is past the critical stage now. She won't die."

The whole story came spilling out about their suspicions, Egg and Binky's reading the material Pastor Lake had on teen alcoholism, and their confrontation just last night with Peggy.

"We were going to talk to Pastor Lake this morning, Mom. You don't think she started to drink more after we'd been to her house, do you?"

Mrs. Leighton shook her head. "Her mother thinks Peggy had been drinking most of the day. I'm surprised she even agreed to talk to you."

"I told you I smelled alcohol on her breath," Egg muttered.

"You mean her mother knew about this?" Lexi asked.

"Mrs. Madison said she and her husband suspected it, but they didn't know what to do. There have been so many difficulties with Peggy lately that they thought she was just depressed, and it was a phase that would pass. I suppose all the signs were there, but no one wanted to believe it."

"Are you *sure* it's not our fault?" Binky's voice was shaky.

"I'm sure of it. But next time, please don't try to handle something this big by yourselves."

A wave of grief swept over Lexi. Her mother was absolutely right. She and her friends tended to try to solve things on their own, going to adults only when all else failed. This time, they'd gone too far. Maybe they'd learned a lesson—the hard way.

"Now what?" Egg looked forlorn and remorseful sitting on the sofa. The command he'd taken of the situation was gone.

"Mrs. Madison is at the hospital now. There are counselors there, but I suggested she call Pastor Lake since he's had experience dealing with cases like this, and could give some spiritual help as well. There's nothing we can do right now except wait—and pray."

———

The next few days seemed to stretch on forever; the hours in school dragged by. Egg, Binky, and Lexi had agreed to tell Jennifer what happened, but asked her not to discuss it with anyone. Things were going to be difficult enough for Peggy as it was. To have rumors and speculation flying around the school would only make it worse.

After discussing the matter with Peggy's parents, Mrs. Waverly agreed to hold Peggy's place as Lady Macbeth for one week. If Peggy was not able to return to rehearsal by then, Mrs. Waverly would have to find someone else for the part. For now, LeAnn Wong was acting as a stand-in for Peggy.

Each afternoon, when Lexi arrived home from school, she would ask her mother if Peggy had called. Mrs. Leighton always shook her head sadly. "Not today." At night, Lexi found herself sitting by the telephone, hoping it would ring.

Was Peggy so angry that she would never speak to them again? Or was she too sick to call? Not knowing made it so much harder to wait.

On Friday evening, as she was cleaning up the kitchen after supper, Lexi heard a knock on the back door. Egg and Binky stood on the steps looking like they'd lost their last friend.

"Come on in. Why the long faces?"

"Have you heard from Peggy yet?" Binky asked.

"Not a thing."

"We haven't either." Binky flung herself onto a kitchen chair. "Do you think she'll ever speak to us again?"

"I've been praying and hoping that she will," Lexi said.

"Oh, I've been doing that too," Binky stated flatly. "Right now, I'm anxious to see some results!"

"Prayers don't always get answered immediately," Lexi pointed out. "I've learned that."

Binky's lower lip protruded in a pout. "It seems to me that God would have a better system for this sort of thing." She crossed her thin arms over her chest. "I can't wait much longer. I feel like I'm going to explode."

"No you won't."

They all whirled toward the screen door at Peggy's voice. She was standing on the step outside. "May I come in?" she asked.

Egg's mouth gaped open, but he recovered enough to pull out a chair for Peggy. She looked pale and withdrawn, but there was a determined look about her at the same time.

"Sit down," Egg offered.

"Can I get you anything? a glass of water? a piece of cake?" Lexi gestured toward the remainder of a cake on the counter.

"Nothing, thank you."

Lexi, Egg, and Binky were at a loss for words, and Peggy didn't seem inclined to talk. After a long, tense moment, she drew a deep breath.

"I've come to apologize," Peggy said quietly.

"Apologize?" Egg asked.

"Yes. For the way I treated all of you the other night. I said some horrible things, and I'm sorry."

"*We* should apologize to you," Egg muttered. "We came barging in on you, making accusations."

"You didn't accuse me of anything that wasn't true," Peggy said softly. "You were right. You caught me doing something I shouldn't have been doing. I'm the one who needs to apologize."

"Are you okay, Peggy?" Lexi asked finally. "We were really scared when your mom called and said you were in the hospital. We thought . . . well, that we might have had something to do with it."

"Oh no." Peggy shook her head. "I was drinking long before you came over." She folded her hands in her lap and sat quietly. She seemed happy just to be with her friends again.

"I was released from the hospital this morning. They told me I could have died from an alcohol over-dose." She looked at each of her friends. "It takes a *lot* of drinking to get to that point."

"Peggy, we just had no idea it was that bad," Binky said.

"No one did. I drank in secret. I loved being alone. I'd just drink all my problems away. It made all the memories of the things that have happened to me drift off. I felt separated from everything and every-one." She gave a weak smile. "I suppose that's why I didn't do so well as Lady Macbeth. It took too much concentration, something I didn't have. All I've done in the past weeks is turn my brain off."

"You don't have to tell us all this if you don't want to, Peggy," Lexi assured her. "We've meddled in your life enough already."

"No, I came here to talk to you. The time I spent in the hospital frightened me—and changed me. I really need to tell you all that's happened, that is, if you don't mind listening."

Lexi saw the determination in Peggy's expres-sion. She nodded and smiled for her to go on.

"I feel like I've been lying to you for such a long time. I want everything out in the open now. Pastor

Lake came to see me every day in the hospital. He's been great. I'm going to be in his support group at the church." Peggy looked ashamed. "I was so ugly at youth group when he was explaining about the new work with teen alcoholics. I didn't want to hear it, of course, because I was drinking, and everything he said was like a knife going into my heart."

Peggy's unexplained behavior finally made perfect sense.

"I don't understand," Binky said. Lexi could tell by the quiver in her voice that she was near tears. "Why *did* you turn to alcohol? I know you've had lots of problems, but it doesn't seem like you, Peggy, to do such a thing."

"I've really felt lost during the past year," Peggy admitted. "It's been the hardest year of my life. I was willing to do anything to wipe out the pain and the memories. Drugs scared me, and I didn't know where to get them anyway. Alcohol was easier to get. I remember the first time I drank. The taste was horrible, and it burned my throat. I wondered how anyone could drink the stuff. Then I started putting the liquor into soda pop to try to disguise the taste.

"It wasn't very long until I was getting up early, before my parents, and going to the liquor cabinet for a drink. Pretty soon I needed it just to get ready for school."

Binky's face showed her disbelief. "Before school? Ugh!"

"I know. It sounds terrible now, but I'd begun to enjoy the way it felt going down. Pretty soon, I decided I couldn't get through the school day without something to drink."

Lexi remembered the time in the costume room. How stupid she felt. How naive she'd been!

"Sometimes I took beer to school, but that smelled too much," Peggy admitted. "So I took a little metal flask I'd found in my dad's drawer and filled it with whiskey."

"You were drinking in the school?" Binky was shocked.

"It wasn't hard. I'd just ask to be excused to go to the restroom. I'd never go in there between classes, because it was too crowded. Sometimes I'd get the guys at the park to buy me miniature bottles of liquor so I could keep them in my school bag. It's amazing how easy it is to get alcohol. Now I'm amazed at how much I thought I needed it."

"Where were we when all this was happening?" Egg asked mournfully. "We should have been helping you."

"It's a nice thought, Egg, but you couldn't have helped me. You couldn't fix the things that were making me drink. Every morning I woke up feeling guilty about Chad's suicide. When I drank, all the guilt and worry melted away. Alcohol helped me cope with or forget the problems I couldn't handle."

"But it didn't take the problems away," Lexi pointed out.

Peggy nodded. "No, but it drowned my feelings and numbed the pain."

"You talk like this is all in the past," Binky observed. "Does this mean you're never going to drink again?"

"I wish I could promise that, but I can't. The doctors, my parents, even you guys, told me I needed help. Now I'm convinced that I do. Pastor Lake seems to understand the things I'm going through. He says that the support group will see me through the bad times. I hope he's right."

Peggy looked very small, young and vulnerable. "My life has been a mess. But I want to get it back on track. With God's help, my friends and family, I plan to take the first steps."

Chapter Eleven

Lexi parked her father's car by the curb in front of the Winston house. She sat for a moment with her hands on the steering wheel, staring down the street. She had a bad case of butterflies in her stomach. This was an important day for Todd and she wanted everything to be perfect.

Lexi climbed out of the car and walked toward the house. Mrs. Winston was at the door waiting. She welcomed Lexi inside.

"Is he ready?"

"He's changed shirts three times and combed his hair so many times I've lost count. It's sweet of you, Lexi, to offer to take Todd to the Hamburger Shack."

"I want his first time out to be a good experience," Lexi said. "The Hamburger Shack is familiar territory."

"You're absolutely right. I think it's a wonderful idea. Returning to school next week won't be quite such a shock to his system."

"What won't be a shock to my system?" Todd demanded as he maneuvered into the foyer. He was using crutches exclusively now and handling them quite well.

121

"We were discussing your trip to the Hamburger Shack," his mother said. "Getting your feet wet, so to speak. When you go to school next week you will already have seen some of your classmates, been out in public a little bit."

"I'm out in public every day I go for physical therapy." Todd eased himself into a chair and laid his crutches on either side of him.

"It's hardly the same thing." His mother laughed and gave him a peck on the cheek.

"I guess you're right. I really do want to try out these sticks, see how people are going to react to them."

Lexi knew that it was still hard for Todd. After being so athletic, it was hard to be dependent on a wheelchair, the walker, and now crutches. No matter how much Lexi tried to reassure him that no one would feel differently toward him, Todd was still unsure of himself.

Lexi dug into the pocket of her jacket and pulled out a pair of bright red ribbons.

"What are those for?"

"Just a little gift."

"A what?" Todd said with a laugh. "They aren't hair ribbons? Do I need a haircut that badly?"

"That's not what I had in mind." Lexi knelt beside him. She tied one of the ribbons in a jaunty bow on one of his crutches.

"What are you doing, Lexi?" Todd demanded.

Lexi tied a similar bow on the other crutch.

"How pretty," Mrs. Winston commented.

"What are they for?" Todd asked.

"They're to make people feel more comfortable

with your crutches. Now they're people friendly. Don't you think it's a good idea?"

Todd looked puzzled and shook his head.

"I was always intimidated by wheelchairs," Lexi explained. "They're cold and mechanical. Worse yet, they remind me of pain, discomfort, handicaps. But once I saw a woman in a wheelchair that was painted bright yellow. There were ribbons and kids' paintings tied all over it. There was even a picture of a funny-faced man in a bow-tie painted on the back. You couldn't help noticing the wheelchair, and it seemed . . . friendly."

"M-m-m-m." Todd still looked doubtful.

"Normally, I wouldn't have walked up to someone in a wheelchair and started talking to them, but I wanted to talk to this lady. If she had such a sense of humor that she could decorate her wheelchair and be happy in spite of her handicap, I assumed she must be a really neat person. It was easy to walk up to her and say, 'I like your wheelchair.' She had a great laugh and an easy smile. I would never have gotten to know her if it hadn't been for her brightly painted chair."

Lexi patted one of the bows and stood up. "That's what these are for. To reassure people. To show them you haven't changed, that you're the same person you always were—friendly and good-natured."

"I think it's an absolutely wonderful idea." Mrs. Winston put her arm around Lexi's shoulders. "You're so clever."

Todd was still staring at the bows as though he weren't quite sure he liked them. "I suppose we can give it a try," he said finally. "But couldn't you have gotten a more masculine color like navy blue?"

Lexi smiled coyly. "It was either baby blue, pink or red."

"Oh. I guess red's okay," Todd said, taking a deep breath. "We'd better go Lexi. It's now or never."

Todd was not very steady yet on steps, but with Lexi's help, he managed to maneuver down them and into the car. Once he was settled, he leaned back in the seat, closed his eyes and sighed.

"Are you all right?"

"No. Not really. I'm a nervous wreck." He opened one eye. "Can you believe it? Me? Worried about going to the Hamburger Shack? I feel like I've been out of circulation for a hundred years; my friends won't be my friends anymore, and I won't even recognize the menu."

"It seems perfectly natural to me," Lexi commented. "Sometimes, when I've missed just a couple days of school, it feels weird going back. It's like a lot of things have happened that I don't know about or understand, and I'm afraid I won't be able to catch up."

"That's it exactly, only multiplied over about a hundred times."

Lexi pulled the car into the parking lot of the restaurant. Todd looked around, unsure of himself. "Lexi, are you sure this is a good idea? Maybe we should just go home and invite some friends over."

"Aren't you feeling well?"

"I feel okay, I guess." Todd looked a little pale. "Just nerves. Maybe I'm not ready for this."

"And you never will be if you don't give it a try," Lexi said matter-of-factly. She jumped out of the car and came around to the other side, opening the door. "You're here now, Todd. At least you have to step inside the building and say hello to whoever is at the counter. Then, if you don't think you can take any more, I'll take you home."

"You drive a hard bargain, Lexi. I didn't know you had such a mean streak."

Lexi smiled sweetly. "Now you do. Come on."

Todd took each step very slowly, but to his surprise he still reached the door of the Hamburger Shack. Lexi pulled it open.

"Give yourself some time. We can always leave if you change your mind." Lexi didn't blame Todd for being nervous. She was sure it did feel strange to be back after all this time. He just needed to walk inside and talk to his friends.

"Todd! Is that you?" Tim Anders jumped up from a table at the front of the restaurant. "I can hardly believe my eyes! You look terrific!"

Jerry Randall rounded the corner of the counter and stood in front of Todd. "You are the best thing I've seen in ages. It's great to have you back, Todd. You look just the same. Hey! I like your crutches."

LeAnn Wong came to stand by Tim. "Foxy bows."

One by one, young people stepped up to greet Todd. He and Lexi made their way slowly between the rows of tables and booths. Brian James nearly fell off his chair when he saw Todd.

Tressa and Gina Williams exited the ladies room directly into his path. "Todd!" they both squealed. "Is it really you?" Impulsively, Tressa grabbed his face and kissed him on both cheeks. Then she blushed at the sight of her lipstick on his face. She dug into her purse and grabbed a tissue to wipe it off, but Todd was laughing too hard to hold still. He was grinning widely by the time he and Lexi reached the booth where Egg, Binky, Jennifer and Matt were waiting.

"We thought you'd never get through all those people," Binky complained.

"That's the most enthusiastic welcome I've ever seen." Matt slapped Todd on the back. "Good to have you back, ol' buddy."

Todd maneuvered himself onto the bench, and Lexi took his crutches and leaned them against a chair.

"Don't put them too far away," Todd instructed, "in case I need to make a quick exit."

"You do a pretty good job of handling those things," Egg observed.

"And I like the bows," Jennifer added.

"You were right, Lexi." Todd winked at her. "The bows were just what I needed."

Jerry Randall took Todd's order first—a hamburger and fries and a banana split, with two spoons. Lexi smiled to herself. It had been a long time since they'd shared a banana split.

"By the way," Jerry said to Todd as he turned to leave. "The boss says your order's on the house. Welcome back."

"Frankly, I think you took pretty drastic measures to get a free burger," Matt joked. "Next time you're that hungry, let me know and I'll buy."

Everyone laughed. It was just like old times. The laughter subsided when the gang saw Peggy Madison walk through the door and head directly for their booth. Todd was the first to speak.

"Hi, Peggy. Good to see you."

"It's good to see *you!*" Peggy smiled. "You're look-ing great."

Peggy's eyes were clear and she looked radiant. In fact, she looked healthier and happier than she had in a long time. "May I join you?"

Lexi made room next to her. "Of course. Sit down."

"Everyone seems a little uncomfortable," Peggy said bluntly. "Is it because of me?"

"No, of course not."

"Don't be silly. . . ."

Each protest seemed a little more artificial than the last.

"It's all right. I understand." Peggy seemed re-laxed and confident. "I just came from my support group meeting," she informed them. "I guess most of you know about that. Pastor Lake says the choice is up to me. I can talk publicly about the problem I've had with alcohol and what I'm doing to resolve it, or I can talk about it only in the support group. But I've decided that I owe it to my friends to tell them what's been happening to me. I've put some of you on a real roller coaster ride, and I'd like to apologize."

"There's nothing to apologize about, Peggy," Egg said gently. "You've been through some tough breaks."

"That doesn't mean I had the right to take it out on you. You've all been great. I couldn't have gotten through the last year without my friends. And you, Todd. Every time I think about what you've been through, it makes me feel guilty."

"Guilty?"

"Well, look at you. You almost lost the use of your legs. But you've been able to cope without turning to drugs or alcohol. I guess I was really weak."

"I had to have some help, Peggy. Not just from all of you, but from God. I have to give Him the credit for pulling me through this."

Peggy nodded. "Well, the least I can do is apologize to all of you for my behavior. And I've decided if there's any way I can help someone else who has a drinking problem, I'd like to do it." She looked around the table. "I realize it's all new to me, but I really want to be a help instead of a hindrance from now on. Does anybody have any questions?"

"How do you know if you're an alcoholic?" Binky asked. "There are lots of teens who think it's really cool to drink, but when do people become alcoholics?"

"According to Pastor Lake, there are people who are social drinkers—they only drink when they are with others who do. Alcoholics generally drink alone, and want to hide the fact. I'd get up in the middle of the night and have a drink. A social drinker would never do something like that.

"And I wouldn't sip a drink, I'd down it like water. Also, my purpose for using alcohol was different than that of a social drinker. I drank in order to drown out my problems. It doesn't make social drinking right, of course, but there is a difference."

Peggy was quiet for a moment, then she looked sheepish. "Do you remember the night Pastor Lake first talked about the teen alcoholics program at youth group?"

"Yes. And you were so uncomfortable," Lexi said.

"Exactly. One of the signs of a real alcoholic is

that he or she becomes agitated when anybody tries to talk to them about their drinking problem. I didn't want to listen to what Pastor Lake had to say. It made me feel angry, guilty and upset. When I started to drink, it was to forget problems. After a while, I wasn't using it to escape memories, but because I enjoyed it and had become dependent on it."

"Peggy, were we right about what you were doing in the park that night after youth group?"

Peggy looked away. "I feel so ashamed. But you were right, Egg. I was buying liquor." She looked at him again, her expression intense. "It's amazing how easy alcohol is to get. At the time, I was so happy to have a source that I didn't think twice about what I was doing."

"Didn't it ever bother you?" Binky asked.

"Plenty of times. Sometimes I'd wake up in the morning knowing that I couldn't remember what had happened to me the night before. I'd have blackouts and not know what I'd done or where I'd been."

"Ooooh, that's scary."

"It is now, when I think about it, sober and in broad daylight. But when you're drunk, you feel as if nothing can happen to you. You feel like your car can drive itself, or that you can fly and no harm will come to you." Peggy shuddered.

"One of the worst days was when I came to rehearsal and did such a horrible job on my lines. I was so scared Mrs. Waverly was going to smell alcohol on my breath. Every time she turned her head away, I popped a couple of mints in my mouth."

Peggy pulled a napkin from the holder and folded it in half. Though she appeared calm, her fingers were trembling.

"I'm really sorry for jeopardizing the play. I had no business drinking before rehearsals. I could have ruined it for everyone."

"It's okay," Binky said. "The understudy's been doing fine, but we still miss you."

Lexi laid her hand on Peggy's arm. "I talked to Mrs. Waverly yesterday, Peggy. She's hoping you'll be able to come back. There's still time."

"Do you think so?" Hope flickered in Peggy's eyes. "I've had the play book at home. I've been trying to memorize my lines, just in case."

"That's wonderful!" Binky was enthusiastic. "You'll be a great Lady Macbeth."

"Well, don't get your hopes up. I've disappointed everyone so far," Peggy said sadly. "Tonight I'm going to rehearsal early. I'll ask Mrs. Waverly for one more chance to redeem myself. If she'll still let me be Lady Macbeth, great. If not, I'll understand. It's her decision."

"It sounds as though you really know where you're going this time," Todd said. "I'm proud of you, Peggy."

"I haven't done anything . . . yet." A smile lit her face. "I do have plans though. Something special that I'm excited about."

"What's that?"

"I've agreed to take part in a program that sends recovering teenage alcoholics into schools to talk to other teenagers. I'm going to tell my story and hope that I can prevent someone else from making the same mistakes. I want something good to come of all that's happened to me. If I can put even one person on the right path, that will be enough for me."

"Won't it be hard, though?" Binky asked. "Standing up in front of other teens and telling them what you did and everything?"

"It can't be any worse than what I've already been through," Peggy said convincingly. "In fact, I see it as some small bit of good coming out of Chad's suicide. Not only will I be able to talk about my own problems with alcohol and the warning signs that accompany it, I'll be able to talk about teenage depression and suicide. Who knows? Maybe somebody who's considered suicide will think twice before ending their own life."

Peggy smiled and spoke evenly. "I really feel like God's calling me to do something for others."

"Wow!" A smile spread over Egg's face.

"And that's not all!" Peggy clapped her hands together. "I almost forgot to tell you about No-Questions-Asked."

They all stared at her blankly, waiting for an explanation.

"Pastor Lake has already asked permission of the high school superintendent to start a No-Questions-Asked ride service. I'm going to try to get together a group of students who have their drivers licenses and access to a car. I'll work up a schedule so that there are two or three drivers on call weekends and week nights."

"On call for what?" Egg asked.

"If someone needs a ride home from anywhere at anytime, they can call No-Questions-Asked. Someone will pick them up wherever they are. If the driver of the car they've been in has been drinking or seems unsafe in any way, or if they've been drinking themselves, they can call and get a safe ride home from No-Questions-Asked.

"It's like Pastor Lake explained to the youth group. Sometimes teens get into dangerous situations because they don't dare call their parents and tell them there's been alcohol at a party. Instead of doing the smart thing by calling their mom or dad to pick them up, they get into the car with a driver who's been drinking or try to drive themselves home.

"No-Questions-Asked will encourage students to call their parents. If they won't, at least there's an alternative. They can call us. Students who volunteer to drive will have to agree not to ask questions— just like the name implies.

"We're going to print a pamphlet that explains what the organization is and how it works. It will also encourage teens to get help if they feel they have an alcohol problem."

"What a great idea!" Todd said.

"I've been thinking of adding some comments of my own," Peggy said thoughtfully. "I know it will be hard to admit to the whole school the problems I've had, but I thought it might help if I added a personal note explaining that I know firsthand that hiding things from your parents leads to trouble.

"I made the mistake of not trusting my parents enough. I don't think we realize how much our parents really care about what we're up to. At least, I wish I'd figured that out earlier. All along I thought I was so smart, and instead, I was being really stupid."

"You're sure not being stupid now," Lexi tried to sound encouraging. "You've got some wonderful ideas. I think No-Questions-Asked could be a good program."

"I hope so, Lexi, I really do. I'd like to make up for some of what I've done." Peggy's eyes began to sparkle. "In fact, I've got some other ideas that I'd like your help with."

"More?" Egg whistled. "You're amazing, Peggy."

"Actually, this isn't my idea, but Pastor Lake's. He suggested that either No-Questions-Asked or another group be formed to help with graduation and prom. He's known several teens who have been in serious car accidents around prom time or on graduation night because they've gone to parties and abused alcohol. He'd like to see a group or an organization host parties that are so much fun and so exciting that students won't even *want* to go to parties where alcohol is being served."

"Does he have some ideas for these parties?" Binky asked.

"He said he'd been to one party at a community fitness center. The center donated the building to the high school for an evening. Everyone played racquetball or tennis, used the weight room and whirlpools. Community grocery stores donated meat and cheese platters, snacks and soda pop. There was good music playing, movies available in another room, board games, ping-pong. Something for everyone."

"Sounds great to me!" Binky said. "I'd go to a party like that."

"That's the idea, Binky. The party would be so attractive, everyone would want to attend. It would make a party where drinking was the main attraction a less desirable place to be."

"So, this group would throw parties like this on prom and graduation nights?" Todd asked.

"Sure, whenever drinking or all-night parties would most likely be an attraction," Peggy answered.

"But what would make people stay all night?" Egg asked.

"Just a lot going on," Peggy said. "You wouldn't have to stay all night, of course.

"Pastor Lake had another good idea to attract teens. Door prizes."

"Hey, sounds great."

"We'd get stores and companies to donate prizes that teens would appreciate, like a walkman or a boom box."

"You mean if you stayed all night you could win a stereo?"

"Something like that."

"That would certainly keep me at a party," Egg said. "When do we start?"

Peggy laughed. "Good thing we still have some time to organize. Spring is a few months away, and we still have to convince the school of our plan. Does this mean I can count on your support?"

"Of course. Count us all in," Lexi said, looking around for approval. "Sounds like a great idea."

Egg and Binky immediately launched into more ideas for No-Questions-Asked and the spring parties.

Lexi felt Todd reach for her hand. It was a wonderful feeling to have both Todd and Peggy here with them again, each on their own personal road to recovery. God had certainly worked His miracles!

Chapter Twelve

It was the final scene. Macduff entered with the gory head of Macbeth. Egg had gone a little overboard with red paint, and it was rather difficult to tell if it was a head or just an over-grown lumpy tomato. Tim Anders, as Malcolm, spoke the final words of the play with gusto:

"We shall not spend a large expanse of time before we reckon with your several loves and make us even with you. My Thanes and kinsmen, henceforth be Earls, the first that ever Scotland in such an honor names. What's more to do which would be planted newly with the time—as calling home our exiled friends abroad that fled the snares of watchful tyranny, producing forth the cruel ministers of this dead butcher and his fiend-like queen, who (as 'tis thought) by self and violent hands took off her life—this, and what needful else that calls upon us, by the grace of Grace we will perform in measure, time and place. So thanks to all at once and to each one, whom we invite to see us crowned at Scone."

Tim exited in a great flourish that nearly toppled him off the stage. Fortunately, the curtains dropped at that moment, saving him from complete humiliation and giving the cast time to gather for their bows.

The audience response was more than any of the cast had expected. As they returned to the stage for the third curtain call, thunderous applause filled the high school auditorium. One by one, parents, friends, and families rose to their feet for a standing ovation.

"You were great! You were marvelous! You were absolutely perfect!" Lexi went from person to person hugging each one and giving out enthusiastic compliments.

The costumes had seemed almost magical on the stage. Matt had been a spectacular Macbeth, and Peggy was a resounding success as his Lady. The three witches had been as believably witch-like as anyone could be. Even Minda was smiling as she came backstage, still wearing the rubber witch's nose with an ugly wart and single hair protruding from it. Lexi flung her arms around Minda and gave her a squeeze. "You were spectacular!"

"I was, wasn't I?" Minda said with a satisfied smile.

Lexi was saved from giving a reply when Egg rushed from the back of the auditorium and onto the stage to congratulate the cast. In his excitement, he tripped on a rope that snaked across the backstage. Then the backdrop, on which everyone had worked so hard, and the castle, made painstakingly of watercolor bricks, began to teeter and topple.

"Someone, catch it!" Matt Windsor, still in his tights and tunic, leaped to the top of the battlement and caught the backdrop just as it was about to fall.

"My hero!" Peggy gave a spontaneous curtsy and fluttered her fake eyelashes at Matt.

He took a deep and gallant bow. "At your service, my Lady."

"How about being at mine?" Lexi interrupted cheerfully, "And hand over those costumes. I want to get them sorted out and hung up before the cast party."

Matt glanced at Peggy. "Is the party still at your house?"

"You bet. It's going to be great! I feel better tonight than I have since . . ." she paused. "I can't remember *when* I felt better than I do tonight! I definitely feel like celebrating."

Lexi threw her free arm around Peggy's shoulders. "You were great, Lady Macbeth. Absolutely phenomenal. The star of the show."

"It was tough," Peggy said with a laugh. "Especially with those three crazy witches hamming it up. They stole the show more than once, didn't they?"

"What did you expect? All the talking in the world couldn't convince Binky that she didn't need dry ice in her witch's pot." Lexi giggled. "A couple of times I thought she was going to disappear in that fog she was stirring up."

"You're coming to the cast party, aren't you?"

"Of course I am. Todd's invited, isn't he?"

"You know it." A shadow clouded Peggy's features. "I wish he'd been well enough to take part in the play."

"There's always next year," Lexi said happily. "Let me get rid of these costumes. We'll see you at your place in a while."

"Egg! Get that lampshade off your head." Binky swatted at her brother. They'd been at the party for some time and Egg was acting weird as usual. Everyone was laughing except his sister.

"I'm trying it on for size," Egg said seriously. "I've always heard about people who go crazy and wear lampshades on their heads, so I thought I'd try it. How does it look?"

Binky studied her brother for a moment. "Actually, it looks pretty good. It covers your entire face. I've changed my mind. Wear it."

Egg pulled the lampshade off. "Are you telling me you don't like my face?"

Binky glared at her brother. "Now Egg, what makes you think I'd tell you something like that?"

"Let's get out of here." Peggy pulled Lexi toward the stairs. "I'm too happy to listen to those two squabble. Peggy's eyes glowed. The whole evening had been a triumphant success.

Happiness has been long overdue for Peggy, Lexi thought.

"Want to sit here awhile?" The staircase appeared to be the only empty spot in the entire house.

"I thought you'd want to go from cast member to cast member rehashing all those wonderful scenes."

"It was a lot of fun and I really enjoyed it," Peggy said, "but, even in this party atmosphere, I can't help thinking about what's happened to me in the past months."

"Plenty, I'd say."

"That's for sure. I'm a whole lot smarter now than

I was a year ago, Lexi." Peggy lowered her voice so only Lexi could hear. "After I'd found out I was pregnant, I thought I was the stupidest person in the world. For a long time, I behaved just like I felt."

"Don't be too hard on yourself."

"I've had lots of struggles, Lexi. Even after I found God, I didn't count on Him as fully as I should have. But, with each experience, I've gotten a little smarter." Peggy stretched her long legs and wiggled her toes.

"One thing I've learned is that God wants us to let go completely. You can't decide to control one portion of your life and let Him have charge of the rest. The commitment's gotta be all or nothing, doesn't it, Lexi?"

Without waiting for an answer, Peggy went on, "Once I learned that, it's made things easier. Now, because of Pastor Lake and the support group, I've finally learned not to worry about next week or next month or next year. I have to live each day and do the very best I can. If I get through a day without taking a drink and without hurting myself or others in some way, I consider it a success."

"You're getting a lot of help from the support group, aren't you, Peggy?"

"Talking to others who have gone through some of the same things I have, and hearing that my feelings are not so foreign to others, has really helped a lot. I've gained tools and hints about handling the problems in my life from those who have seen them work."

Suddenly, chaos broke out around them. Egg came flying through the hallway in hot pursuit of

Minda. He was wearing her rubber witch's nose and cackling wildly.

"Egg McNaughton, you leave me alone. You're too weird," Minda screeched.

"Round about the caldron grove; in the poisoned entrails throw. Toad, that under cold stone days and nights has thirty-one, swelt'red venom sleepy got; boil thou first i' the charmed pot. Double, double, toil and trouble; fire burn, and caldron bubble."

"Leave me alone, Egg. You didn't have to memorize my lines."

"Actually, Egg makes a pretty good witch, don't you think?" Lexi commented after the pair had disappeared into the kitchen.

Peggy nodded, and Lexi looked toward the living room. Binky and Todd were deep in animated conversation. Matt was regaling the lighting crew with a story. Jennifer was lounging comfortably in a wingback chair, accepting compliments like a queen.

Lexi breathed a relieved sigh. All was right in her world again.

———

Minda, Lexi, and their friends take their sense of hearing for granted until they meet Ruth Miller. Ruth, a hearing-impaired girl, teaches them all a difficult lesson. Read Cedar River Daydreams #16, *Unheard Voices*.

A Note From Judy

I'm glad you're reading *Cedar River Daydreams*! I hope I've given you something to think about as well as a story to entertain you. If you feel you have any of the problems that Lexi and her friends experience, I encourage you to talk with your parents, a pastor, or a trusted adult friend. There are many people who care about you!

Also, I enjoy hearing from my readers, so if you'd like to write, my address is:

Judy Baer
Bethany House Publishers
6820 Auto Club Road
Minneapolis, MN 55438

Please include an <u>addressed, stamped envelope</u> if you would like an answer. Thanks.